Longarm had tol_____ about three hours, but it seemed more like three minutes when his eyes snapped open and his senses sprang to full alert. His hand shot out and closed around the butt of the Colt as he rolled over. The gun came up and his finger tightened on the trigger as the barrel lined up with the dark shape that stood just inside the door of the room.

"Custis!" Deborah Kane cried out in alarm.

Longarm held off firing, but just barely. His pulse hammered in his head as he brought his instincts under control. "Good Lord, gal!" he burst out. "I damn near shot you!"

Deborah came closer to the bed. "I'm sorry. I didn't mean to cause a problem, Custis. I just . . . had to see you again . . ."

"You know that word of this is going to get around, don't you? It ain't gonna help your reputation, you being a widow lady and all."

Deborah smiled. Longarm could see her face in the light that filtered in through the thin curtains.

"Maybe we'll be lucky," she said as she moved closer to him. "Maybe we'll all be wiped out, and I won't have to worry about my reputation."

Longarm chuckled at the dark humor and put his arms around her. He was powerfully drawn to her too, and if he was going to die, there were worse ways to spend some of his final moments on earth . . .

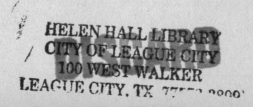

DON'T MISS THESE
ALL-ACTION WESTERN SERIES
FROM THE BERKLEY PUBLISHING GROUP

THE GUNSMITH by J. R. Roberts
Clint Adams was a legend among lawmen, outlaws, and ladies. They called him . . . the Gunsmith.

LONGARM by Tabor Evans
The popular long-running series about Deputy U.S. Marshal Custis Long—his life, his loves, his fight for justice.

SLOCUM by Jake Logan
Today's longest-running action Western. John Slocum rides a deadly trail of hot blood and cold steel.

BUSHWHACKERS by B. J. Lanagan
An action-packed series by the creators of Longarm! The rousing adventures of the most brutal gang of cutthroats ever assembled—Quantrill's Raiders.

DIAMONDBACK by Guy Brewer
Dex Yancey is Diamondback, a Southern gentleman turned con man when his brother cheats him out of the family fortune. Ladies love him. Gamblers hate him. But nobody pulls one over on Dex . . .

WILDGUN by Jack Hanson
The blazing adventures of mountain man Will Barlow—from the creators of Longarm!

TEXAS TRACKER by Tom Calhoun
J. T. Law: the most relentless—and dangerous—manhunter in all Texas. Where sheriffs and posses fail, he's the best man to bring in the most vicious outlaws—for a price.

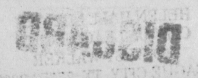

TABOR EVANS

LONGARM

AND THE HANGTREE VENGEANCE

DISCARD

J

JOVE BOOKS, NEW YORK

THE BERKLEY PUBLISHING GROUP
Published by the Penguin Group
Penguin Group (USA) Inc.
375 Hudson Street, New York, New York 10014, USA
Penguin Group (Canada), 90 Eglinton Avenue East, Suite 700, Toronto, Ontario M4P 2Y3, Canada
(a division of Pearson Penguin Canada Inc.)
Penguin Books Ltd., 80 Strand, London WC2R 0RL, England
Penguin Group Ireland, 25 St. Stephen's Green, Dublin 2, Ireland (a division of Penguin Books Ltd.)
Penguin Group (Australia), 250 Camberwell Road, Camberwell, Victoria 3124, Australia
(a division of Pearson Australia Group Pty. Ltd.)
Penguin Books India Pvt. Ltd., 11 Community Centre, Panchsheel Park, New Delhi—110 017, India
Penguin Group (NZ), 67 Apollo Drive, Rosedale, North Shore 0632, New Zealand
(a division of Pearson New Zealand Ltd.)
Penguin Books (South Africa) (Pty.) Ltd., 24 Sturdee Avenue, Rosebank, Johannesburg 2196,
South Africa

Penguin Books Ltd., Registered Offices: 80 Strand, London WC2R 0RL, England

LONGARM AND THE HANGTREE VENGEANCE

A Jove Book / published by arrangement with the author

PRINTING HISTORY
Jove edition / January 2008

Copyright © 2008 by The Berkley Publishing Group.
Cover illustration by Miro Sinovcic.

ISBN: 978-0-515-14397-3

JOVE®
Jove Books are published by The Berkley Publishing Group,
a division of Penguin Group (USA) Inc.,
375 Hudson Street, New York, New York 10014.
JOVE is a registered trademark of Penguin Group (USA) Inc.
The "J" design is a trademark belonging to Penguin Group (USA) Inc.

PRINTED IN THE UNITED STATES OF AMERICA

10 9 8 7 6 5 4 3 2 1

Chapter 1

Longarm smelled the smoke before he saw the light.

He reined his horse to a halt and swung down from the saddle. The night was very quiet, and sound could travel a long way out here on the prairie. Better to approach the place on foot, he decided.

Since there were no trees or even any bushes to tie the reins to, he left the horse ground-hitched and hoped the animal was well trained enough to stay where he left it. That was one drawback to renting horses or picking them up at army remount depots: Often, he didn't know the tendencies of the animals he rode.

But he couldn't do anything about that now, so he had to take a chance. He slid the Winchester from the saddle boot and started forward, cat-footing through the buffalo grass with an easy grace that was unusual in a man as big as he was.

The moon was only a sliver that cast little light. A Comanche moon, they called it down in Texas. Maybe up here in western Kansas they called it a Cheyenne moon, but Longarm didn't think so. He had never heard that term anyway.

But there were plenty of stars, millions of them, in fact,

and as Longarm returned his thoughts to the job at hand, the glow from those celestial beacons helped him spot something on the prairie a couple of hundred yards away. A deeper patch of darkness in the gloom, and as he crept closer, he realized it was a soddy, a homesteader's shack made of blocks of earth stacked on top of each other like bricks to form the walls. In a land with few trees, that was about the only kind of house a settler could build.

The soddy had no windows, and the door was closed, but enough of a gap remained around the door to let a little light escape from inside. Longarm saw it, and figured the smoke he smelled came from the tin stovepipe that no doubt stuck up through the earthen roof. Even though the night was uncomfortably warm, a fire was going in the stove. Maybe whoever was inside was cooking a late supper.

Or maybe the sodbusters had company. Unwelcome company . . .

Longarm had no way of knowing yet if Tom Rankin was in there. He had been tracking Rankin for a couple of days. The man was wanted for a series of train robberies and stagecoach holdups in which he had looted the U.S. mail. That made his crimes federal offenses, which explained why a deputy United States marshal was after him.

That wasn't all Rankin had done, of course. He had been arrested by a local lawman in a settlement south of here and locked up in the town's cracker-box jail. The local badge had seen reward dodgers on Rankin and knew that Uncle Sam's boys wanted him, so he'd sent a wire to Billy Vail, chief marshal of the First District Court of Colorado, at Vail's office in Denver, and Vail had dispatched Longarm to pick Rankin up and bring him back there.

But by the time Longarm reached the town where Rankin was being held, the outlaw had escaped from jail, in the process killing the star packer who had arrested him. His trail had led north.

Now Longarm suspected that Rankin had stopped at

that soddy to water his horse and beg a meal from the homesteaders who lived there. If they cooperated, Rankin might move on without hurting them. But if they put up a fight, Rankin was capable of taking whatever he wanted and then murdering them.

Of course, thought Longarm as he continued his stealthy approach, if he busted in to arrest Rankin, that would put the sodbusters in danger too, because Rankin would likely fight back and then there would be a gun battle. If hot lead started flying around inside that soddy, it wouldn't be any too careful about who it hit.

Might be better to just keep an eye on the place, wait, and see what happens, he decided as he went to one knee about fifty yards away from the soddy. When Rankin left, Longarm could jump him then.

The aroma of food being cooked drifted to his nostrils and reminded him of how long it had been since he'd eaten. His stomach was starting to think that his throat had been cut, and the smell of some sort of savory stew didn't help matters any. Longarm reached into his shirt pocket and found one of his three-for-a-nickel cheroots. He clamped it between his teeth and left it unlit. That didn't help much, but it was better than nothing, he supposed.

He had been kneeling there for about ten minutes when a gun roared inside the soddy.

Longarm's teeth bit through the cheroot as he surged to his feet. He uttered a heartfelt "Damn!" as he broke into a run toward the soddy, holding the Winchester at a slant across his chest. If Rankin had started murdering the inhabitants, Longarm couldn't just stand by and do nothing. He worked the rifle's lever, throwing a cartridge into the chamber.

No more shots sounded in the seconds it took for Longarm to cover the distance to the soddy. Without slowing down much, he lifted his right foot and slammed the heel of his boot against the door, next to the latch. As the door burst open, Longarm's momentum carried him on into the shack. He dropped to a crouch, swiveling from side to side as he looked for his quarry.

He shouted, "Hold it, Rankin!" as he spotted the outlaw on the far side of the soddy's single room. Another man lay facedown on the floor near Rankin's feet. A dark blood-stain spread on the back of his coarse, homespun shirt.

Rankin's gun was back in its holster. He must have thought the danger was over once he'd killed the sodbuster. With the muzzle of Longarm's Winchester centered on his chest, he didn't dare reach for the gun on his hip.

"Damn it," Longarm ground out. "You shot him in the back."

"No," said a woman's voice from behind him. "I did."

Then something smashed against the back of Long-arm's head, driving him forward into blackness. He didn't feel it when he hit the hard-packed dirt floor, because he was already out cold.

Chapter 2

The darkness didn't last long. As Longarm crawled up out of it, he sensed that he had only been unconscious for a few moments. And unlike other times in the past when he had been knocked out, his memory was clear. He knew exactly what had happened when he burst into the soddy.

He had been a damned fool, that's what had happened. That bitter thought loomed in his brain.

And yet, he couldn't take all the blame. Rankin had been traveling alone since escaping from the jail where he'd been locked up. Longarm was sure of that because he had talked to several witnesses who had seen the fugitive. There was no way Longarm could have known that Rankin was joining up with a confederate—let alone a female confederate—at this lonely soddy.

He realized he shouldn't have allowed anyone to get behind him like that, but as far as he had been aware, Rankin was the only threat inside the shack. Well, live and learn, he told himself as those thoughts flashed through his head along with returning consciousness.

He hoped he would live anyway, but that was sort of up in the air at the moment.

"Shouldn't I go ahead and shoot him before he wakes

up?" asked the woman's voice. Despite that disturbing question, Longarm was careful to keep his eyes closed and his face expressionless. He wanted Rankin and the woman to think that he was still out cold.

"No, not yet," replied Rankin. "I want to see who he is first. He yelled my name when he came in. Must be a lawman of some sort."

Longarm heard the scrape of boot leather on the dirt floor as Rankin came over to him.

"Point that gun at his head," Rankin went on. "If he moves, you pull the trigger, understand?"

"I understand," the woman said. "But what if you're in the way? I don't want to shoot you."

"I won't be in the way."

Longarm remained motionless. That gal already had an itchy trigger finger. The question she had asked about going ahead and shooting him proved that. He didn't want to do anything that would spook her into firing.

He felt Rankin lift the Colt from the cross-draw rig on his left hip. It was damned hard for Longarm to let himself be disarmed that way. Under the circumstances, though, he still thought it best to bide his time and wait for the right moment before making his move.

Rankin's hand went into the pocket of Longarm's shirt and found the leather folder that contained his badge and bona fides. Rankin pulled the folder out, and a moment later the outlaw grunted in surprise.

"This bastard's a deputy U.S. marshal," he said. "Name of Custis Long. Hell, when he came busting in here, I thought he was some sort of crazy Indian at first."

This wasn't the first time somebody had mistaken Longarm, with his high cheekbones and skin tanned to the color of old saddle leather, for an Indian. The sweeping longhorn mustache sort of gave it away that he wasn't, though.

"Once I thought about it, I realized he must be a badge

6

toter," continued Rankin. Longarm heard the rustle of clothing as Rankin straightened from his crouch. "All right, you can shoot him now if you want. Or I will, if you'd rather that I do it."

Longarm was ready to tense his muscles and try to roll out of the way of the shot, even though the odds were against him being able to do that, when the woman said, "I don't know if I want to."

"Then move back out of the way—"

"No, I don't mind shooting him. But before I do, you got to promise me you'll take me with you, Tom."

"Hell, I already said I would, didn't I?"

"I mean all the way to San Francisco. A girl likes to know she's going to be taken care of. Besides, I already shot my husband, and now you want me to murder a stranger, and a lawman to boot. It's not too much to ask for a promise that you won't just up and abandon me somewhere."

Longarm had a hard time keeping the surprise off his face, but he managed. He'd had no idea that the woman was the wife of the dead sodbuster on the floor. Rankin had been a few hours ahead of him on the trail. During that time, the outlaw must have arrived at this shack, played up to the woman, and convinced her that he would take her away from this harsh, lonely life.

Longarm knew that more than one woman had gone mad from the isolation out here on these wind-swept plains. Obviously, this gal had been willing to do whatever it took to get away, up to and including gunning down her husband and throwing in with a wanted desperado.

But figuring all of that out didn't do Longarm a bit of good. He was still faced with the danger of having either Rankin or the woman shoot him, so he was going to have to make his play . . .

That was when somebody groaned, and the woman screamed.

7

Longarm's eyes snapped open. He surged up onto hands and knees, then powered onto his feet. The woman was to his right, Rankin to his left. In front of him was the woman's husband, the wounded homesteader Longarm had taken for dead.

The man was still alive, though, and he groaned again as he tried to push himself upright. Rankin and the woman had both turned toward him when he made the first sound. Rankin even said, "Shit! He's still alive!" before he spotted Longarm moving from the corner of his eye.

The woman was closer. Longarm swept his right arm around in a backhand that caught her on the jaw and sent her sailing backward to crash into the wall of the soddy. During his boyhood back in West-by-God Virginia, he had been taught not to hit girls, but since she had already pistol-whipped him and then talked so calmly about killing him, he reckoned he could make an exception this once.

Even before the woman hit the wall, Longarm lunged at Rankin. The outlaw was trying to get his gun out. The fingers of Longarm's left hand wrapped around Rankin's right wrist, pinning it to his side with the gun only half drawn. Longarm swung his right fist in a looping punch, but Rankin jerked his head aside so that the blow only grazed him above the ear and knocked his hat askew.

Rankin grabbed Longarm around the neck and wrestled with him. The two men staggered across the floor as they grappled. Longarm's feet tangled in something, and as he felt himself falling, he realized that he had tripped over the legs of the wounded sodbuster. Rankin went down too, still trying to choke Longarm as he fell.

They landed on a chair that collapsed under them. Longarm rolled and hauled Rankin along with him. Feeling heat, Longarm realized he was next to the cast-iron stove. With a heave and a shove, he thrust Rankin's shoulder against the hot metal.

Rankin screamed as the searing heat burned through his

8

shirt. That loosened his grip on Longarm's neck. Longarm drove the heel of his hand under Rankin's chin and forced the outlaw's head back. Another roll put Rankin on the bottom and Longarm on top. Balling his right hand into a fist, Longarm smashed it twice into Rankin's face, causing the man's head to bounce off the hard-packed dirt of the floor. Stunned, Rankin went limp. Longarm had knocked all the fight out of him, at least for the moment.

That left the woman to deal with. Longarm hadn't forgotten about her, but dealing with Rankin had almost taken too long. The woman had recovered her wits and still had hold of a gun. It was an old cap-and-ball pistol that probably belonged to her husband, Longarm saw as he turned toward her. The barrel shook some as she jabbed it toward him, but at this range she could hardly miss, no matter how shaky she was.

Longarm dived to the side as she fired. The roar of the gun was deafening in the close confines of the soddy. Longarm didn't know where the bullet went, but he was pretty sure he wasn't hit. He scrambled to his feet.

The old pistol was a single-action weapon, which meant the woman had to pull the hammer back and cock it before she could fire again. She had both thumbs looped over the hammer and was struggling to pull it back when Longarm grabbed the gun and wrenched it out of her hands. She cried out. He didn't know if she was hurt or just scared or both, and right now he didn't care. He pushed her back against the wall and said, "Damn it, settle down!"

Then he flipped the pistol around in his other hand, eased back the hammer, and leveled the gun at Rankin as the outlaw started trying to get up. Rankin still looked groggy and maybe not completely sure of what was going on, but he seemed to understand clearly enough as Longarm snapped, "Don't move, Rankin, or I'll blow your damn brains out!"

Longarm would have done it too. He was mad at this

unexpected complication in his effort to bring Tom Rankin to justice.

Keeping Rankin covered, he backed across the room until he reached a point where he could watch both the outlaw and the woman. He saw that Rankin's gun had slipped out of its holster while they were wrestling on the floor. It lay there on the dirt, not right next to Rankin but within easy reach.

"Don't even think about making a play for that gun," Longarm warned him. "I don't mind taking you back to Denver with a bullet hole in your head, old son. Easier that way, in fact."

"Take it easy, Marshal," Rankin said in a voice taut with tension. "I'm cooperating with you."

Longarm grunted. "Yeah, until you get a chance to pull some trick. Scoot away from that revolver."

Rankin complied. Without looking at the woman, Longarm added, "Ma'am, move over there next to him."

Her chin lifted in a defiant jut. "Why should I?" she demanded.

"Because I got half a mind to shoot Rankin in the knee just to make things simpler, and I don't reckon you want any more blood spilled on your nice clean floor."

Although, come to think of it, she hadn't minded spilling her husband's blood, Longarm reminded himself.

"All right," she said. "All right, I'm going. Don't hurt him."

Longarm smiled, but his eyes remained cold and humorless. "Looks like the lady's a mite smitten with you, Tom."

"Do I know you?" Rankin asked in a sullen voice.

"Nope. Never laid eyes on you until tonight. But I know who you are, and I know what you're capable of."

Bitterly, Rankin glared at Longarm and said, "You never would've been able to turn the tables on us if not for that other bastard."

"This lady's husband, you mean?"

"Zach and I were married," the woman said, "but he was never really a husband to me." Her tone was dull and lifeless now. "He was just a taskmaster. All he cared about was me doing the chores he gave me. He . . . he never made me feel like a real woman."

"So you jumped at the first chance you got to run away with a stranger and shot your husband in the back," Longarm said. It wasn't a question.

The defiance was back on the woman's face as she said, "He had it coming. He didn't make me happy."

Longarm glanced at the sodbuster, who had slumped on the floor again. The man's head was twisted now so that Longarm could see his face, and he saw that the man's eyes were glassy and devoid of life. The luckless bastard had regained consciousness for a moment and tried to get up, but then death had gone ahead and claimed him.

The distraction that had provided had been lucky for Longarm, though, and the big lawman's long years in a hazardous profession had taught him one thing:

Take your luck where you can find it, because it may not come around again.

Chapter 3

Longarm was still faced with the problem of what to do with
Rankin and the woman. She had moved over beside the outlaw. Longarm asked her, "You got any rope around here?"

She glared at him. "I'm not going to help you."

"Not even if I promise to take you to San Francisco if
you do?"

Hope lit up her eyes for a second; then her gaze fell as
she realized he wasn't serious. Longarm then felt a little
bad about the gibe. But she had murdered her husband on
a cold-blooded whim, he reminded himself, so he wasn't
going to waste a lot of time feeling sorry for her.

He glanced around the inside of the shack, never taking
his eyes off the prisoners for more than a heartbeat, and
found some old pieces of rope in a corner along with some
other trash. The homesteader had probably used the rope to
help hold his old plow together when it tried to come apart.
Sodbusters had hard lives, no doubt about it.

Longarm tossed the rope across the room and told the
woman, "Tie his hands behind his back."

"This won't do you any good, Long," Rankin said with
a sneer on his face. "You can't hold me. No lawman and no
jail ever has."

13

"We'll see," Longarm said. Bluster was cheap, and he didn't care to engage in it.

With a sullen look on her face, the woman picked up one of the lengths of rope. She wasn't bad-looking, in a weather-beaten way. Her curly hair had started out fair, and the sun had bleached it even more until it was almost white. The lines of her body in a worn, tight-fitting old cotton dress told Longarm that she was relatively young, maybe twenty-five or so. After another five years out here, she probably would have looked fifty.

Tom Rankin was a medium-sized hombre with black hair and dark, cruel eyes. The scars of some childhood illness pocked the lean cheeks of his face, but despite that he was still a handsome man in a way. The homesteader's wife must have thought so anyway. Or maybe she didn't even care what he looked like. Maybe when she looked at him, all she saw was escape from a hard, dreary existence.

At gunpoint, Rankin put his hands behind his back and allowed the woman to lash his wrists together. Longarm kept a close eye on her and made sure she pulled the knots tight. Satisfied that Rankin wouldn't be able to get his hands loose without a lot of work, Longarm ordered him to sit down.

"You mean here on the floor?" Rankin looked offended.

"That's right," Longarm told him. "Put your back against the wall and slide down, then stick your legs out in front of you."

Grudgingly, Rankin complied with the orders. Longarm told the woman to use another piece of rope and tie Rankin's ankles together. She did that, and as she straightened from the task, she shot Longarm a venomous look and asked, "What now? Are you going to knock me out and tie me up?"

"Only if you make me," said Longarm. "Turn around and put your hands behind your back."

She looked like she was going to argue with him, but

after a second she sighed and did as she was told. Longarm set the old pistol on the table, where he could reach it in a hurry, and tied her wrists.

"What's your name?"

"Go to hell," she muttered. "What business is it of yours?"

"I sort of like to know who I'm arresting for murder."

A little shudder ran through her. Then her back and shoulders jerked, and Longarm realized she was crying.

"My . . . my name is Mollie," the woman said. "Mollie Bramlett. My husband was . . . was Zach Bramlett."

Longarm didn't trust her for a second, but the tears rolling down her cheeks and the anguished look on her face seemed genuine enough. Maybe she'd had a few tender feelings left for her husband, even though she had hated him enough to put a bullet in his back a short while earlier.

She had to know too that after tonight her life would never be the same. Her actions had changed things forever, and there was no way to put them right again. That was enough to make somebody cry right there.

Or maybe she was just trying to make him feel sorry for her. If that was the idea, she was going to be mighty disappointed.

"Wh-what are you going to do with me?" she asked through her tears.

"Sit down over there," Longarm said, pointing to the chair that hadn't been busted up during the fight with Rankin.

"No, I mean . . . are you really going to arrest me?"

"You admitted you shot your husband."

"I'm sorry! I . . . I wasn't thinking. I was just so tired of being stuck out here in the middle of nowhere . . . and Zach treated me so bad . . . that when this . . . this man offered to take me away . . ."

"In case you didn't know it," said Longarm, "this

hombre is a wanted outlaw. A killer. And you'll notice, he ain't denying what I said about him."

Rankin laughed. "I don't pretend to be something that I'm not, Marshal."

Mollie Bramlett ignored him and said to Longarm, "If you'll let me go, I'll never hurt anybody again. I'll leave this place and go back to St. Louis."

"That's where you're from?"

"That's right. Zach and I met there. He . . . he came to the house where I worked. You know what I mean."

Longarm nodded. Like a lot of frontier wives, Mollie had started out as a prostitute and had married a man she probably didn't know well at all, just to get away from that life.

But she had wound up in a life she liked even less, and this time she had killed to escape.

"Sorry," said Longarm, and in a way he supposed he actually meant it. "There's a settlement north of here. Dry Creek, I think it's called. I'm taking the two of you there. There'll be a jail to lock you up. It'll be up to the State of Kansas to try you for your crime, ma'am. Murder is a state charge, not a federal one. Rankin's going back to Denver with me."

"It's a long way to Denver," Rankin said with a cocky grin. "You'll never get there with me, Marshal."

"Keep talking like that and I'll take you back facedown over the saddle instead of sitting in it," Longarm warned.

Rankin still looked smugly confident, but he didn't say anything else. Mollie Bramlett sat down in the chair like Longarm told her to, and he tied her to it so she couldn't get up. Then he checked Rankin's bonds and found that the outlaw was tied securely. Even so, he didn't breathe a sigh of relief. He wouldn't do that until a door with iron bars clanged shut with Rankin on the other side of it.

And even then, he wouldn't get careless about things.

Longarm picked up his Colt and slid it back into its

holster. He laid his Winchester on the table. He unloaded the old cap-and-ball pistol and placed it on the table as well. Then he pulled a blanket off the bunk in a corner of the room and draped it over the corpse of the sodbuster.

"You're going to just *leave* him there?" Mollie asked.

"I'll bury him in the morning before we start out," Longarm explained.

"You mean I'm going to have to sit here and . . . and look at him all night?"

Longarm shrugged. "You're responsible for him being that way, I reckon. Don't look at him if you don't want to."

A pot of stew was still simmering on the stove. Longarm found a bowl and dipped some of it out. There was no chair besides the one Mollie was tied to, so he ate standing up. As he did, he wondered just how things had happened in here. Had anything been said or done to let Zach Bramlett know that his wife was leaving him? Or had she just shot him down from behind without warning?

Longarm didn't know and didn't suppose it mattered. The poor bastard was just as dead either way.

"Let me go," Mollie said. "Let me go and . . . and I'll make it worthwhile for you, Marshal. I don't have any money, but I'll do anything you want."

Longarm just shook his head. "Right now, ma'am, you don't have anything that I want. Except maybe another bowl of this stew. It's been a mighty long time since breakfast."

Chapter 4

It was a long time until daybreak too, but Longarm stayed awake all through the interminable hours. He sat cross-legged on the dirt floor, on the other side of the soddy from Rankin and Mollie, with the Winchester across his lap. Both of the prisoners dozed off from sheer exhaustion, but Longarm's hazardous profession had trained him to remain alert for long stretches of time. A man's life might depend on his ability to do that.

Come morning, his muscles were stiff and sore and his eyes felt like they had been plucked out of his head, coated with sand, and then shoved back into their sockets. He blinked away some of the discomfort and stretched out some of the kinks, then untied Mollie from the chair. He lifted Rankin from the floor. Then he marched both of them out of the shack and told them, "If you take off running, I reckon you'll find that you can't get out of sight before I come back out of the soddy. I'm a good shot with this Winchester, and I'll knock your legs out from under you. I'm sorry to say that goes for you too, ma'am."

Then he went inside and dragged out Bramlett's blanket-shrouded body. He found a shovel in the shed where the sod-buster kept his mule, and started digging a grave. Rankin

19

and Mollie stood by watching. Neither of them had tried to escape. Out here on this trackless prairie, there weren't many places to hide.

Rankin grinned as Longarm labored on the grave and the burial. Mollie looked away, unwilling to watch the grim task, and Longarm didn't see any point in forcing her to witness her late husband being laid to rest. When it was done, and the mound of dirt had been tamped down as best he could, he started figuring out how he was going to get his prisoners to the nearest settlement.

Rankin's unsaddled horse was in the shed with the mule. Longarm slapped the saddle on the animal and led it around to the front of the soddy.

"You get the horse," he told Mollie. "Rankin, you can ride the mule."

"That jughead doesn't have a saddle," Rankin complained. "His spine will cut my balls to pieces."

"Too bad. I reckon you can walk to Dry Creek if you'd rather."

Rankin cursed under his breath, but didn't argue anymore. Mollie's feet were already free. Longarm didn't loosen the bonds on her wrists. He helped her step up in the stirrup and then swing her leg over the horse's back. She flushed with embarrassment at the undignified position, but it couldn't be helped.

Getting Rankin on the mule was trickier. Longarm had to cut his feet loose, then told him to climb up on an empty crate. He held the mule while Rankin sprawled awkwardly on the beast's back.

Longarm's horse was grazing about a hundred yards from the soddy. Longarm went to get him and led him back by the reins, then mounted up.

"Don't we get anything to eat before we start out?" Rankin asked.

"The law in Dry Creek will feed you, I expect, once you're locked up," said Longarm.

"Not even any coffee?"

Longarm gestured with the Winchester's barrel. "Get moving," he ordered.

He wasn't sure how far it was to the settlement, so as their mounts plodded northward over the prairie, he asked Mollie, "How long does it take to get to Dry Creek?"

"When Zach would take the buckboard to town for supplies, he'd usually start first thing in the morning and not get back until a long time after dark." Her voice was dull. "He'd leave me out here by myself all that time, at the mercy of wolves or Indians or any other varmint that came by. Said I might as well be working while he was fetching supplies."

"I didn't see a buckboard around the place."

A bitter twist pulled at Mollie's lips. "That's because Zach had to sell it to buy more seeds. He wasn't a very good farmer. He lost more crops than he ever grew."

Longarm nodded. With Rankin mounted on the mule, especially without a saddle, the three of them couldn't move much faster than Bramlett would have been able to in the buckboard, so that meant it would probably be sometime after noon before they reached Dry Creek. He found himself thinking about a big meal, a few cups of coffee laced with dollops of Maryland rye, and a comfortable bed. All that might be waiting for him once he got his prisoners behind bars.

But for the time being, thinking about those things didn't amount to much more than torturing himself, so he shoved the thoughts out of his head, concentrating instead on riding and keeping an eye on Mollie and Rankin.

There wasn't much to see out here, just mile after mile of flat, grassy plains. The monotony was broken only by an occasional soddy that marked the location of some lonely homestead. The line that marked the westward progress of the farmers was back to the east. A few sodbusters had ventured this far, but not many. This area had been cattle coun-

try at one time, but most of the big ranchers had moved farther west and north, into Colorado and Wyoming. The
Cheyenne and the Pawnee had been pretty well pacified, so
it was only a matter of time until this region would be covered with farms, thought Longarm, but that time had not
yet come.

So this was a lonely place, and a man could ride for
miles without seeming to get anywhere. The only real
change that was visible to mark the passage of time was
overhead, as the sun rose higher in the sky, reached its
zenith, and then started its long slide down to the western
horizon. Its brassy heat slid around the riders like thick liquid.

Longarm's eyes snapped open. He hadn't realized they
were closed. Rankin and Mollie were still riding in front of
him, so they hadn't realized that he'd dozed off either.
Rankin muttered curses under his breath, but Mollie rode
in stoic silence.

Longarm gritted his teeth. It wouldn't do for him to fall
asleep again. To keep his mind occupied, he started thinking about a gal he knew back in Denver. Her name was
Lorna Hammett, and she worked in the Denver Public
Library, a place that Longarm liked to frequent, especially
toward the end of the month when his funds were running
low and payday was still a ways off. Lorna was a smart,
pretty, brown-haired woman, a mite on the short side but
with enough curves to more than make up for that.

She was also just about the horniest gal Longarm knew,
and she was endlessly inventive in the ways she could
come up with for him to ravish her. One time she might
want to give him French lessons while she rubbed herself
off, the next she might get on hands and knees, stick her
ample backside in the air, and ask him to put it to her that
way. Sometimes she even wanted to do it normal-like.

However Lorna wanted it, Longarm was glad to
oblige . . . and when they were through, they could talk

22

about almost anything under the sun, because in addition to being randy all the time, Lorna also read more than anybody else Longarm knew. She was a damned good friend, and now as he rode across the Kansas plains, he found himself missing her something terrible. He vowed to himself that he would go and look her up just as soon as he got back to Denver.

Well, as soon as he could after he made sure that Tom Rankin was in the federal lockup, he amended.

In the meantime, while thinking about Lorna Hammett had chased away his drowsiness, as he'd intended, it had also left him with a mighty stiff cock and nowhere to stick it. He shifted in the saddle, trying to ease the discomfort in his denim trousers.

As he looked past Rankin and Mollie, he spotted some dark spots on the prairie up ahead, and when those spots drew closer and resolved themselves into several men on horseback riding toward them, that took Longarm's mind off his predicament. He didn't know who they were likely to run into out here. Probably just some cowboys from one of the cattle spreads still operating in the area, but until Longarm knew for sure that the strangers didn't represent a threat, he was going to remain watchful.

It was a good thing that he did, because a moment later, with whoops and hollers, the riders suddenly spurred toward Longarm and his prisoners, and puffs of smoke jetted into the air as the crackle of gunfire reached Longarm's ears.

Chapter 5

"Those bastards're shooting at us!" yelled Rankin.

Longarm had already figured that out. However, from the sound of the shots, the men were using handguns, and Longarm and his prisoners were still out of effective range for such weapons.

Not for the Winchester, though. Longarm pulled his horse to the side so that he could aim past Rankin and Mollie, and brought the rifle to his shoulder.

Not knowing who the men were or why they were shooting at him, Longarm didn't really want to kill any of them. So he aimed high as he cranked off a couple of rounds, sending the bullets over the heads of the onrushing gunmen.

They didn't stop shooting. They didn't even slow down.

So Longarm bit back a curse, lowered his sights, and blew one of the varmints out of the saddle.

The crack of the rifle was followed almost instantly by the sight of one of the men tumbling backward off his horse as Longarm's bullet slammed into his chest. That got the attention of the other three men, all right. They reined in, bringing their mounts to skidding halts, then whirled the horses around and went back the other way, pausing only to pick up the fallen man and fling him over his now-empty saddle before resuming their flight.

Longarm let them go. The odds were still three to one against him, so if the strangers were willing to give up the fight, so was he.

"What the hell was that about?" asked Rankin.

Longarm shook his head as he thumbed three fresh cartridges through the Winchester's loading gate to replace the ones he had expended. "Your guess is as good as mine," he said. "Let's go."

Rankin twisted around on the mule's back to stare at him. "If we keep going north, that's the direction those bushwhackers went! They could double back. We're liable to ride right into another ambush."

"Maybe," admitted Longarm, "but Dry Creek is in that direction, and it's still the closest settlement in these parts." He glanced up at the sun and tried to judge how much time had passed since they'd left the Bramlett homestead. "Fact is, it can't be too far off now."

"But those men—"

"Looked like they were taking off for the tall and uncut," Longarm said, breaking in on Rankin's complaint. "They must not have any rifles, and when they realized that I do, they decided they'd have to pay too high a price to get close enough for their Colts to make a difference. Don't get ahead of yourself, Rankin. Best way to eat an apple is one bite at a time."

Rankin mentioned something the big lawman could do with an apple, but since he expressed the obscene and probably physically impossible sentiment under his breath, Longarm let it pass. The outlaw faced front again and banged his feet against the mule's flanks, kicking the animal into motion.

Mollie had gone through the incident without seeming to get excited or scared. Her expression remained dull and uncaring. Maybe she was feeling overwhelming guilt over the fact that she had murdered her husband, thought Longarm. But it was more likely that she was just sad over the fact that she wasn't going to get to run off to San Francisco after all. She had traded the grinding monotony of life as a sodbuster's wife for the equally unappealing prospect of spending the rest of her days behind prison bars. It wasn't much of a swap as far as Longarm was concerned.

Longarm saw a splash of red on the grass where the man he had shot had fallen. They rode on past the spot, and as they continued moving northward, they didn't see any more signs of the men who had attacked them. About an hour later, they came in sight of a line of trees running east and west. Those trees marked the course of a stream, and as Longarm, Rankin, and Mollie rode closer, Longarm began to make out the shape of buildings as well. He spotted a church steeple.

That had to be Dry Creek, he thought. And the presence of trees, even scrubby cottonwoods like these appeared to be, meant that the stream that had given the settlement its name wasn't dry after all, at least not the whole year 'round.

Rankin glanced back over his shoulder. His eyes were wider now, and Longarm thought he saw panic stirring in them. The realization was soaking in on the outlaw that he was very close to being locked up again, and getting closer with each passing moment. Rankin had probably hoped for a chance to get away during the trip to Dry Creek, but that opportunity had never arisen. The closest thing had been when those strangers on horseback attacked them, and that incident had been over almost before it began.

"I know what you're thinking, Rankin," warned Longarm. "You're wondering what your chances would be of me missing with this Winchester if you made a break for it. Well, you go right ahead and give it a try if that's what you want to do, old son. Wouldn't bother me a bit."

Longarm's confidence was all the answer Rankin

27

needed. His shoulders slumped as he looked forward again. A grim smile touched Longarm's mouth as he saw that reaction.

The settlement of Dry Creek was located mostly on the south side of the stream, although Longarm saw a few houses on the far side. The main street paralleled the creek and was three blocks long. The church and the nicer homes clustered toward the western end of town, while businesses took up the central part. The eastern end was where the saloons, the gambling halls, and the whores' cribs were located, along with some shacks and slightly nicer cabins. A lot of frontier towns had a definite line of demarcation where the respectable part of town changed over to the not-so-respectable. That didn't appear to be the case in Dry Creek. The change was more gradual here.

Longarm steered his prisoners toward the central block, figuring that was where the local lawman's office would be located. He hoped Dry Creek had a decent jail. If not, he might have to lock Tom Rankin in a smokehouse or storage shed or something like that. He would put Mollie Bramlett in a hotel room if he had to.

Before they reached the street, Rankin said, "Listen, Marshal. I can put my hands on eight thousand dollars if you'll let me go. It's loot that I've cached from jobs in the past. It's all yours if you want it. I'll take you to it if you'll let me ride away from there."

Longarm frowned. "What'd be stopping me from lying to you, letting you lead me to that loot, and then throwing you in jail anyway?"

"I guess I figure you're . . . an honest man." Rankin gave a hollow laugh. "Which means you wouldn't let me bribe you in the first place, right? I guess I didn't think that through long enough."

"I reckon not," said Longarm. "Keep moving."

Rankin shook his head. "Honest men," he said, as much

to himself as to Longarm. "How the hell can you deal with somebody like that?"

Longarm didn't figure that was worthy of an answer, so he didn't give one to Rankin. The three riders rounded the corner of a large, two-story building that, according to the sign over the porch, housed the Plaza Hotel. Longarm wasn't sure how the place had gotten that name, since there was no plaza here in Dry Creek. He supposed the proprietor had liked it, for one reason or another.

As he reined in and called to the others to do likewise, Longarm realized that something had been bothering him about the settlement as they approached. Now, as he looked both ways along the street, he knew what it was. Nobody was moving around. Horses were tied at the hitch racks and wagons were parked here and there, but he didn't see any people on the boardwalks or the porches of the buildings. Dry Creek wasn't a ghost town. There were people here; the saddled horses were proof of that.

But for some reason they were all lying low, staying inside somewhere.

Longarm's frown deepened as he felt eyes watching him. Something was definitely wrong here, and his instincts made him wonder if those strangers who had been so trigger-happy were connected with it. He spotted a building at the far end of the block with a sign hanging from the boardwalk awning that read MARSHAL'S OFFICE. Heeling his horse into a walk, Longarm pointed with the barrel of the Winchester and ordered his prisoners, "Down there."

As they rode up to the marshal's office, which was located in a squat building made of sod and timbers, the door suddenly swung open and a voice called from inside, "Hold it right there! Don't come any closer, or I'll shoot!"

The twin barrels of a shotgun were pointed straight at Longarm, Rankin, and Mollie.

Chapter 6

Longarm heard fear in the man's voice. Keeping his own voice as calm and level as he could, he said, "Take it easy, friend. We're not looking for trouble, and we don't mean any harm to anybody here in your town."

It was a guess that the man holding the Greener was Dry Creek's marshal, and Longarm thought that was a pretty strong possibility. That hunch was confirmed a moment later when the man stepped out on the porch.

He was a tall, barrel-chested man on the far side of middle age, with a rugged, weathered face and a white mustache. A battered tin star was pinned to his vest. He kept the shotgun trained on Longarm and the two prisoners as he asked, "Who are you, and what are you doin' here?"

"Name's Custis Long," replied Longarm. "I'm a deputy U.S. marshal out of Denver, and these two are my prisoners." With a short motion of the Winchester's barrel, he indicated Rankin and Mollie.

The local star packer frowned. "The woman too?"

Longarm nodded and said, "The woman too. She killed her husband."

"What about that hombre?"

31

"He's Tom Rankin. You might have some reward dodgers on him. He's wanted for train robbery and murder and breaking jail."

"I reckon you can prove what you're sayin'?"

Longarm had recovered the folder with his badge and bona fides after Rankin had taken it from him in the soddy. Carefully, he reached in his pocket now, withdrew the folder, and tossed it on the porch at the marshal's feet.

"There's my identification."

"This ain't a trick, is it?" demanded the local lawman. "Because if it is . . . if you're workin' for Torrance . . . you'd better know that this Greener's got a hair trigger, and I ain't afraid to use it."

He was sure afraid of *something,* though, thought Longarm. "I don't know anybody named Torrance," he said. "And that's the truth."

Keeping an eye on the visitors and one hand on the shotgun, the marshal bent over and reached down with his other hand to pick up the folder. He straightened, flipped it open, and grunted as he glanced at the badge and identification papers inside.

"I reckon you're who you say you are, all right," he said as he finally lowered the scattergun. "Better get down and come on in . . . even though it might be smarter and safer if you was to turn around and light a shuck outta here."

"You heard what the man said," Longarm told Rankin and Mollie. "Let's go inside."

He swung down and helped them dismount since their hands were tied, Mollie first and then Rankin.

As they took the single step onto the porch, Longarm asked, "You've got cells where I can lock them up, Marshal?"

"I've got one cell," said the local lawman as he returned Longarm's bona fides. "That's all."

Longarm nodded. "We'll put Rankin in it then." He prodded the outlaw in the back with the muzzle of the rifle. "Get moving."

The lone cell inside the marshal's office appeared to be secure enough. It had only one small, high, barred window in the rear wall, which was built of thick, sturdy timbers that must have been freighted in from somewhere. The door was made of iron bars. There was no cell block; the cell door opened directly into the marshal's office.

With a sigh, Rankin went into the cell. Longarm followed him, took a clasp knife from his pocket, and used it to cut the ropes around Rankin's wrists. Rankin rolled his shoulders gratefully as he brought his hands around in front of him. He started rubbing them together and winced. Longarm knew that had to be caused by the pain of the returning blood flow to the outlaw's hands.

Longarm backed out of the cell and slammed the door. The marshal came over, thrust a key into the heavy lock, and turned it. "There you go," he said to Longarm. "Ain't nobody ever busted out of that cell, and I don't expect this hombre to start."

"I'm glad to hear it." Longarm thrust his hand out. "And I'm much obliged for the help, Marshal."

"Frank Webber," the lawman said, introducing himself as he shook hands. "I'd say that I'm pleased to meet you, Long, but the truth is, I ain't. I got enough to worry about right now without bein' saddled with a couple of prisoners."

"They're *my* prisoners," Longarm said, trying not to sound annoyed. Marshal Webber's attitude rubbed him the wrong way.

"Yeah? What're you plannin' to do with them?"

"Well, I thought I'd make arrangements for the county sheriff to come and pick up Miz Bramlett here," Longarm said as he nodded toward Mollie. "She'll have to be tried in

33

a local court for killing her husband. And I'll take Rankin back to Denver with me to face federal charges."

"Send for the sheriff." Webber grunted. "That's a good'un. So's that idea about takin' Rankin back to Denver."

Longarm's irritation finally spilled over. "Marshal, what are you talking about? What's going on here? Ever since we rode in, I've gotten the feeling that this whole blamed town is scared to death."

"That's because—" Webber stopped and shook his head. "Let me ask you a question. Did you run into any trouble on the way here?"

"Matter of fact, we did. Some fellas on horseback charged us, shooting and yelling as they came."

Webber nodded. "Cy Torrance's men. What happened? How'd you get away from them?"

Longarm hefted the Winchester and said, "They were out of pistol range when they jumped us, but that didn't stop them. I fired a couple of warning shots over their heads, and when they kept coming, I ventilated one of them."

Webber grimaced and asked, "Kill him?"

"Maybe. From the looks of the way he tumbled out of the saddle, probably."

The local lawman gave a solemn shake of his head. "That was just about the worst thing you could've done. Those were just tryin' to turn you back and keep you from comin' on into town. That's what you should've done, turned around and got the hell out while you still had the chance. Now Torrance will have it in for you too."

"Who the hell is Cy Torrance?"

"He was the first cattleman in this part of the state and still owns the biggest spread. He's used to runnin' things his own way in these parts and gettin' whatever he wants."

"And what is it he wants?" asked Longarm.

"Dry Creek," replied Webber in a hollow voice. "He wants this town."

"You mean he wants to take it over and run everything himself?"

Webber shook his head. "No. He wants the town dead. He wants to burn it to the ground and kill every man, woman, and child in it."

Chapter 7

For a moment, Longarm could only stare at Webber in amazement. He glanced over at Mollie and saw that her eyes were wide with interest as well. The local lawman's unexpected words had finally shaken her out of her stupor.

"Hold on there, old son," Longarm said. "You mean to tell me that this hombre Torrance wants to wipe out the whole blasted *town*?"

Webber nodded. "That's right. He's got a big crew, and he's sent his men out to ride a big ring around the settlement and keep anybody from going in or out. It's been that way since early this morning. That's why I was so surprised to see you folks. I didn't expect Torrance's hands to let anybody through." A humorless chuckle came from him. "I'll bet old Cy really lit into the bunch that failed to turn you back."

Longarm shook his head. "No offense, Marshal, but this is loco. I saw telegraph wires leading into town. Why don't you just . . ." His words trailed off as understanding dawned on him. "Torrance's men cut the wires, didn't they?"

"Yep. The line went dead just before Cy rode into town this morning and told us what was going to happen."

"He *told* you?" That sounded loco to Longarm too.

Webber nodded again. "Sure. Wouldn't be near as good for him if we didn't know what was gonna happen. Tellin' us was part of his revenge."

"Revenge for *what*?"

Webber opened his mouth as if to answer, then stopped and shook his head. "It don't matter," he muttered. "What's important is that you might still have a chance to get out of here, Marshal. Torrance's men have orders to shoot to kill if anybody leaves town, but you might make it through if you've got a fast enough horse. Probably have to fight your way out." He shrugged. "Chances are they'll kill you, but any chance is better than none, I reckon."

Longarm frowned in thought as he considered the suggestion. He tugged at his right earlobe, then scraped his thumbnail along the line of his jaw. "And if I did get clear, I could bring back help," he mused.

"Not in time to help us," said Webber. "Torrance didn't say when he was gonna hit the town. That's another part of his vengeance, I reckon, makin' everybody wait and sweat. But I figure it'll be tonight. Tomorrow night at the latest. The county seat's a day's ride, and the nearest army post is farther than that." He shook his head. "No, we're on our own here, Marshal. Torrance has got us pinned in good and proper."

Rankin had been listening intently from inside the cell. Now he grasped the bars of the door and said, "Damn you, Long! What in blazes have you gotten us into here?"

"Shut up," said Longarm. "This is none of your business."

"The hell it ain't! You heard that old pelican. That fella Torrance plans to wipe out the whole town and burn it to the ground! You really think he's gonna spare us just because we weren't here when whatever it was happened to put such a big burr under his saddle?"

"He might have," said Webber, pulling at his chin, "if you hadn't shot one of his riders, Long. Now he'll feel justified in killin' the three of you too."

Rankin tried to shake the bars, but they didn't budge.

"Lemme out of here! Damn it, I didn't do anything to Torrance! I deserve a chance to try to get out of here too!"

Longarm swung angrily toward the cell. "You're forgetting that you're under arrest, Rankin," he snapped. "You're going back to Denver to face justice for your crimes."

"Haven't you been listening? Nobody's getting out of here unless we go *now*!"

"And that'd be a long shot," Webber put in. "Like I said, Cy's got the town surrounded."

Longarm glared at the local lawman and asked, "So what are you going to do? Just sit here and wait for him to ride in and massacre everybody?"

"No, we'll fight back when the time comes. I've got men posted on several of the roofs in town, keepin' an eye out for trouble. They saw the three of you ridin' in and let me know somebody was comin'. I didn't know what to hope for. It was already too late for you to get out, but in a way I hoped you'd just ride on around town and keep goin', so I wouldn't have to tell you that you're fixin' to die."

Mollie let out a moan as she stood there and shook for a second. Then, she turned and plunged toward the doorway.

Longarm had seen the panic growing stronger and stronger inside her, and was ready for her when she tried to dash out of the marshal's office. He took a fast step and looped an arm around her, pulling her back.

"Hold on," he told her. "You're not going anywhere."

"We have to get out of here!" she said in a high, ragged voice. "They're going to kill us all! We have to get out!"

Longarm took her over to an old sofa that sat along one wall of the office, next to a potbellied stove. He pushed her down onto the cushions and said, "Stay right there. It's not going to do any good to run around like a chicken with its head cut off."

Mollie turned so that she was sitting sideways, leaned her face against the back of the sofa, and began to sob quietly.

Longarm figured she was thinking that things just kept going from bad to worse for her.

But the situation didn't look too good for any of them. He turned back to Webber and asked the local lawman, "Any chance that somebody might be able to talk some sense into Torrance's head?"

"None at all, I reckon. If you tried, you'd just wind up dyin' sooner." Webber sighed. "No, Cy loved that boy of his. Talk won't do any good. It's too late for that."

"Don't you think you'd better tell me exactly what's going on here?" suggested Longarm, his voice low but intense.

Webber thought it over and then nodded. "I don't see how it could hurt anything now. It's shameful, though. Purdee shameful."

"Go ahead and spit it out."

Webber hesitated, and then said, "I'll do better than tell you. I'll show you. First, though, I reckon we ought to do something with the lady."

Longarm reined in his impatience to find out what had happened here in Dry Creek to doom the entire town. He said, "I figured on taking her down to the hotel and locking her in a room there, if you didn't have enough cells."

"That'll do," agreed Webber. He reached for his hat, which sat on his scarred old desk. "Come on. I'll go with you. Might make things a little easier."

Longarm grasped Mollie's arm and helped her to her feet. She was still crying, but not making much noise about it. He led her out of the building. The three of them walked down the block to the Plaza Hotel.

Several men with rifles in their hands stood in the lobby. They looked like they were ready for trouble as Longarm, Webber, and Mollie came in. One of the men asked, "Who are these people, Frank?"

"This here's Marshal Long, a federal lawman out of Denver," replied Webber.

Hope lit up the faces of the men. "You've come to help us, Marshal?"

"Now how could that be, Everett?" asked Webber before Longarm could say anything. "We didn't even know what Cy Torrance had in mind until this mornin', and it was too late to send for help then because his boys had already cut the telegraph wires."

The townsman's expression fell. "Yeah, that's right," he admitted.

"Marshal Long was just passin' through with a couple of prisoners," Webber went on. "We got the fella locked up down to the jail, but he needs a place to put this lady."

"She's a criminal?" the man called Everett asked with a frown.

"Accordin' to the marshal, she murdered her husband."

"Wait a minute," said one of the other men. "I recognize her. That's Mrs. Bramlett. I sold some supplies to her husband a while back. He's dead?"

Longarm nodded. "That's right."

The townie let out a whistle of surprise. "Well, what do you know about that?"

Longarm said, "How about that room?"

"Of course," Everett said. "This is my hotel, Marshal. I'll be glad to help out. I have several vacant rooms upstairs."

"Good locks on the doors?"

"Yes, certainly. The best that money can buy."

"What about the windows?"

"Well, no, they don't lock. But I suppose you could nail them shut."

Longarm thought it over for a second and then nodded. He didn't like the idea very much because fire was always a danger in any wooden structure, but the hotel was only two stories tall. If he left Mollie in a room with unlocked windows, she might risk climbing out and jumping.

"You got a handyman who can do that?" he asked Everett.

41

The hotel owner nodded. "Yes, I do. Room Seven is vacant. I'll tell him to get a ladder and a hammer and some nails and get to work on the window. That room has only one."

"That'll be fine," Longarm told him. "And I'm much obliged, Mr. Everett. I'll watch the prisoner until that's taken care of."

Longarm escorted Mollie up the stairs, along with Everett, who showed them where the room was located. It was on the side of the hotel, overlooking an alley, with no balcony outside. That was another point in its favor, thought Longarm.

The hotel handyman was a gangling young fellow who leaned a ladder against the outside wall, climbed up it, and drove a couple of nails into the window frame, fastening it securely to the sill so that it couldn't be raised. That took about ten minutes. When the chore was finished, Longarm cut the ropes on Mollie's wrists. She wasn't crying anymore, but she whimpered a little as pins and needles flooded through her hands and fingers. She collapsed onto the bed and lay with her back toward Longarm.

"I'll bring you some food later," he told her, but she didn't give any sign that she heard him.

He left the room. Everett locked the door and handed the key to Longarm. "I suppose you'll want to keep up with this, Marshal."

"Thanks for your help."

"I'm glad to do it." Everett smiled, but there was no humor in the expression, only sadness. "It takes my mind off what we're all facing here. Do you know what happened?"

Longarm shook his head. "Your marshal said he'd tell me, though."

"It was a terrible thing," murmured Everett. "Just terrible."

The two of them went downstairs to the lobby, where Webber was talking to the men who were there. One of them said to Longarm, "You have to do something to help us, Marshal. It's your duty as a peace officer."

"Before I can do anything, I've got to know what's going on here," Longarm said with a meaningful look at Webber.

The local lawman sighed. "I said I'd explain, and I will. Come on." He looked at the other men. "You boys stay here, and be on the lookout for trouble. I don't expect Cy to try anything until after dark, but you never know."

They nodded in agreement, but looked nervous. Longarm couldn't blame them for that. They were storekeepers and hotel owners, not fighting men. Living on the frontier always held risks, but evidently the situation here in Dry Creek was out of the ordinary.

When they left the hotel, Webber nodded toward the trees and said, "Let's take a walk down by the creek."

Longarm went with him, and as the two men walked along the street, he had that feeling of being watched again. The citizens of Dry Creek were all huddled inside the buildings, waiting for all hell to break loose.

As Longarm and Webber approached the creek, Webber pointed to one of the cottonwoods. "See that?" he said. "There on that branch?"

Longarm's eyes narrowed as he said, "I see a piece of rope tied to it. Looks like it's been cut on the end. Is that . . . ?"

Webber nodded. "Yep. That's where we did it. That's where we hanged Cy Torrance's boy, Harry."

Chapter 8

Longarm's eyes narrowed as he looked over at Webber. "Are you talking about a lynching?"

"Sad to say, I am." The marshal scowled. "But by God, we thought he had it comin'! I've never seen this town so upset and outraged."

"Wait a minute," said Longarm. "You *thought* he had it coming?"

Webber grimaced and looked away. "Yeah. Come to find out . . . Well, I don't really like to talk about it . . ."

"Sort of late to be worried about being embarrassed now, isn't it?"

"You've got to understand. The whole town sort of looked out for Sarah. She didn't have no family. After her folks died, we took her in. She was sort of like, hell, I don't know, everybody's little sis."

Longarm held up a hand and shook his head. "I've got a feeling this is a long story, and I need something to eat and a cup of coffee. You have a good café in this town?"

Webber's expression brightened a little as he nodded. "We sure do. Miz Kane runs it. Come on. We'll get you a surroundin', and I can tell you all about it, even though it's gonna shame me to say it."

They turned away from the cottonwood that still had part of the hangrope attached to it, although as they walked off, Longarm cast one glance over his shoulder at the grim reminder of what had happened here. Webber led him to a small frame building across the street from the marshal's office. A sign on the building simply announced CAFÉ. Whoever ran the place didn't put on any airs.

The café wasn't doing much business. None, to be precise. No customers sat at the tables with their neat, blue-and-white checked tablecloths or on the stools arranged along a counter. A woman stood behind the counter, wearing a blue gingham dress and a white apron. Brown hair fell around her shoulders. She was around thirty, Longarm judged by the small lines around her mouth and eyes. Not beautiful maybe, but definitely pretty. She didn't smile as Longarm and Webber came in, but she gave them a solemn nod of greeting.

"Hello, Marshal," she said. "What can I do for you?"

"Howdy, Miz Kane," said Webber as he gave the brim of his hat a polite tug. "I wasn't sure if you'd be open for business today."

She shrugged a little and laughed. "Why not? Some people might want a last meal that they don't have to fix for themselves."

Longarm didn't like the tone of fatalistic resignation he heard in her voice. That attitude seemed to grip the entire settlement, and it rubbed him the wrong way. He had never been the sort to just give up and accept whatever fate seemed to have in store for him. He would rather fight, even if he lost in the end.

The woman looked at him and asked, "Who's this?"

Webber made the introductions. "Custis Long, this is Miz Deborah Kane. Ma'am, this here is Marshal Long. He's a federal lawman from Denver."

A brief flare of hope appeared in the woman's pale blue eyes. "You've come to help us?" she asked Longarm. Like everybody else in this town, she wanted help. They wanted somebody to come in and save them from the consequences of what they had done.

But maybe he was judging folks too harshly, he told himself, so he kept his voice cordial as he said, "No, ma'am, I'm afraid not. I just happened to ride in and find that you folks have got yourselves in a heap of trouble."

Her eyes flared again, but with anger this time. "Don't blame all of us," she said. "Some of us thought that hanging Harry Torrance without a trial was the wrong thing to do, even if he was guilty of what he was accused of."

"Blast it, Deborah," Webber said. "Sarah said before she died that he done it. What else did you expect anybody to think?"

She shook her head. "She said Harry's name. She never said he was the one who hurt her."

"But I asked her who done it, and she answered Harry."

"Yes, well, we know that she was wrong, don't we? She might not have even understood what you were asking her, Frank."

Webber sighed. "I guess you're right about that. Hell, I know you are. Beggin' your pardon for the language."

Deborah smiled and said, "Under the circumstances, I have more important things to worry about than a little cussing. Like how my daughter and I are going to live through this mess you and the others have gotten us into."

Webber rolled his shoulders and shook his head, looking a little like a bear as he did so. "Marshal Long wants somethin' to eat and some coffee."

"I can fix you up," Deborah said to Longarm. "Have a seat anywhere. There's not going to be a supper rush today."

"I'll have a cup of coffee too," said Webber, "if, uh, that's all right."

After a second, Deborah nodded. "Sure, Marshal."

Longarm and Webber sat down at one of the tables.

Deborah poured the coffee and brought it over, then went through a door behind the counter into the kitchen. When she came back a few minutes later with a plate piled high with food, she was accompanied by a little girl about ten years old, with blond pigtails. The youngster carried a plate full of biscuits. Despite the difference in hair color, Longarm saw a resemblance between Deborah and the little girl and knew the girl had to be the daughter Deborah had mentioned.

"Go back into the kitchen and play, honey," Deborah said as they placed the plates on the table.

"All right, Mama," the girl said. She gave Longarm a shy smile, and then left the room as her mother had told her.

Without being asked, Deborah pulled out one of the empty chairs at the table and sat down. In a low voice, she said, "Go ahead and tell Marshal Long what happened, Frank."

Webber took a sip of his coffee and nodded. He still looked reluctant, but as Longarm gratefully dug into the plate of steak, potatoes, and beans, Webber said, "First, you got to understand about Harry Torrance. As the son of Cyrus Torrance, the biggest rancher in this part of the state, Harry was just like his old man: used to getting his own way."

Longarm nodded. "I figured as much. Who's this Sarah you mentioned?"

"Sarah Gilley. A pretty girl about sixteen. Long blond hair and sweet as apple pie. We don't know for sure how old she was, because she was, uh, not quite right in the head."

"She and her mother and father were all sick with a terrible fever when they came to Dry Creek," Deborah added. "We think they were coming out here to homestead, but we're not even sure of that. The parents were too far gone to make any sense, so the only reason we know their names was because of some letters we found in their wagon."

"Lord knows how that fella managed to keep his team movin', as sick as he was," Webber went on. "But he did, and when they got here, he fell off the wagon seat, right in the middle of the street. Folks came a-runnin' to help, of course, and we found Sarah and her ma in the back of the wagon. We don't have a doctor here, but we done what we could for all three of 'em." He shook his head. "Sarah's ma and pa didn't make it. They both died that night. But Sarah was able to pull through."

"We nursed her back to health," said Deborah. "Just about everybody in town helped. It took her a long time to recover. And when she did . . . her mind wasn't right. Even though she was fourteen or fifteen at the time, her mind was that of a child even younger than my daughter, Lucy. Maybe she was that way to start with, or maybe the fever was responsible. Lord knows how high it was at its worst. Her face was just blistering to the touch, almost."

"That's a real shame," Longarm said. "But it's good that she had you folks around to take care of her."

Deborah nodded. "We tried to. She was healthy again, and sweet as could be, as Marshal Webber said. She moved in with Reverend Collier and his family."

"Everybody in these parts looked out for her," said Webber. "Even the cowboys on the spreads around here treated her with respect. They didn't try to take advantage of her 'cause she was slow, and they must've thought about it, because she was mighty pretty."

Longarm made a grim guess. "But then something happened to her."

Both of the other people at the table nodded. Deborah glanced at the door to the kitchen, making sure it was closed so that her daughter couldn't hear before she said, "That's right. Sarah was raped one night, about a week ago.

The man who did it beat her too until she was almost dead. She only lived a few minutes after someone found her."

"It was a fella named Barney Whitten who worked down at the stable as a hostler," said Webber. "I was makin' my rounds, and Barney came runnin' up and told me somethin' terrible had happened to Sarah. He was cuttin' through an alley on his way home after work when he practically tripped over her, he said. We ran back to where she was, and I seen right away that she was in mighty bad shape." Webber had to swallow hard before he could go on. "So I asked who hurt her, and she said Harry's name. Said it plain as day. I picked her up and carried her back to my office and sent Barney runnin' all over town lookin' for help. A lot of people showed up, includin' Deborah here, but there was nothin' anybody could do. Sarah died less'n an hour later. She never said another word after claimin' that it was Harry Torrance who'd hurt her."

"Was Torrance in town that night?" asked Longarm.

Webber nodded. "He was. When I got Sarah back to the office, I went lookin' for him and found him in the Prairie Saloon. He had just gotten there, though. Said he'd ridden into town about ten minutes earlier. There was a scratch on his face. When I asked him about it, he said he'd gotten it from a cottonwood branch while he was fordin' the creek in the dark."

"But you thought Sarah gave it to him when she was fighting back against him," said Longarm.

"Well, shoot, it stood to reason, didn't it? He was around, he looked like he'd been in a tussle, and Sarah herself said he was to blame for what happened to her. I didn't have no choice but to arrest him."

"How'd he take that?"

"He didn't cotton to it," said Webber. "Put up a fight, in fact, and I had to clout him over the head with my gun. I hauled him down to the office and locked him up in the same cell where that Rankin fella is now. He cussed me out

50

and said his pa would have my hide. Said I'd be mighty sorry for what I'd done. Nobody got away with treatin' Harry Torrance like that, he said."

"Called himself by name like that, did he?"

"Yeah."

Longarm nodded. From everything Webber had said, he knew the type, all right. Cruel, arrogant, and high-handed, accustomed to running roughshod over folks until he got whatever he wanted, and furious whenever anyone defied him. Longarm had no doubt that Harry Torrance had been exactly that way.

But that didn't mean he had raped and murdered Sarah Gilley.

"Some of Cy Torrance's riders were in town that night," Webber went on. "They rode back out to the ranch and told Cy what had happened. He was in town first thing the next mornin', bellerin' like a bull and demandin' that I let his boy out of jail. I told him I couldn't do that and that Harry would have to stand trial for killin' Sarah Gilley. Cy said I'd be sorry. And the way it turned out, that's the truth. I'm just as sorry as I can be."

Longarm made another guess. "Because it turned out that Harry Torrance wasn't guilty after all . . . but you hanged him anyway and didn't find out until later that he hadn't done anything."

Webber didn't say anything, and neither did Deborah Kane.

But their silence was all the answer that Longarm needed.

Chapter 9

The grim quiet hung over the table for several moments before Webber continued with the story. The coffee in his cup was growing cold now, forgotten as he talked.

"People got worried about what Cy Torrance would do," said Webber when he finally resumed. "We've got a circuit judge who comes around every six weeks or so, but it was gonna be several weeks before it was time for him to get here. I thought about tryin' to take Harry to the county seat and keepin' him there, but I knew if I rode out with him, Torrance's boys would take him away from me. And I knew that if I kept him in my little jail, Cy would ride in with his whole crew and take him out of there. Even if Harry somehow made it to trial and was found guilty—and you'd likely have a hard time findin' twelve men in these parts who'd go on record as votin' to convict him, for fear of what Cy might do to get back at them—we all knew he'd never hang. His pa wouldn't allow it." Webber clenched his right hand into a fist and tapped it on the table several times. "Everybody in town knew all this. Everybody."

"So you got together and decided to take action while you still could," said Longarm.

Webber didn't meet his eyes. "That's right. We had a meeting. Just about every man in town was there."

"And so were some of the women," Deborah put in. "Some of us even argued against lynching Harry, but we were shouted down."

"It wasn't really a lynching," insisted Webber. "We took a vote."

"A vote isn't the same thing as a trial," Longarm pointed out.

"You don't have to tell me that. I know it. But that's what happened, and it was decided to carry out justice while we still could, before Cy had a chance to bust Harry out of jail. A group of men came for Harry later that night and Lord help me, I . . . I let them take him."

"And they strung him up on that cottonwood."

"Yeah. He kept yellin' that he didn't do it, but nobody paid any attention to him."

"What did his father do when he found out?"

"Well, that was sort of surprisin'. Cy didn't do anything at first. Oh, he was mad, sure enough. I heard later that he got drunk, took a pistol, and shot out damn near every window in his ranch house, he was so crazy mad. But he stayed out on his spread and didn't come into town. He just sent his foreman and some of his hands in with a wagon to bring Harry's body back. Jess Garth, that's Cy's foreman, he cut the body down. Said for us to leave the rest of the rope on the branch, so we wouldn't forget what we'd done. Said if anybody touched it, he'd come back and kill the man who took it down. Then they took Harry home and buried him out there on the ranch, next to his ma. Harry was the only child she and Cy ever had."

"To tell you the truth," said Deborah, "I believe Mr. Torrance really thought that Harry was guilty. Even though Harry was his son, deep down he had to know what sort of man he was."

Longarm nodded. He suspected that Deborah was right.

Even though he had no youngsters of his own, he could understand how a parent would know what a child was capable of, although that parent might not want to admit it, even to himself.

"So you think he held his temper in check because he believed that Harry killed that girl," said Longarm. "But then he found out different."

"We all did," said Webber with a heavy sigh. "A couple of days ago, old Eph Bridges, the fella who owns the stable, found Barney Whitten in there, hung from one of the rafters. Barney threw the rope over the rafter, put the noose around his own neck, and kicked the stool he was standing on out from under him. Barney could write a little. He'd left a letter sayin' that he was the one who killed Sarah and that he couldn't stand it anymore, knowin' what he'd done and knowin' that Harry Torrance died because of him too."

"What about Sarah identifying Torrance as her killer?" asked Longarm.

"Well . . . she never actually *said* Harry's last name. I asked her who done it and she just said Harry. He's the only one in these parts with that name. But Barney . . . you never met Barney, so you wouldn't know this . . . Barney had this big bushy beard and this wild head o' hair . . ."

"Good Lord," said Longarm. "She said *hairy, h-a-i-r-y*?"

"That's all we can figure."

Longarm sat back in his chair, astounded. A man had been lynched—and that was what it was, no matter what Webber wanted to call it now—and a whole town had been put under a death sentence because of such a simple misunderstanding.

Longarm let it soak in on him for a minute before he said, "How did Torrance find out?"

"We don't know for sure," replied Webber. "My guess is that somebody who wanted to get on Torrance's good side rode out to the ranch and told him. But that just made things move a mite faster than they would have otherwise.

Cy would've found out sooner or later. You can't keep a thing like that quiet forever."

Longarm nodded, knowing that the local marshal was right. When people knew a secret, especially something as shameful as this, somebody talked about it. Somebody always talked. Lawmen counted on that quirk of human nature.

"What did Torrance do when he heard about Whitten's confession?"

"He and some of his men rode into town early this mornin'," Webber said. "Soon as I seen Cy's face, I knew somethin' was bad wrong. He looked even worse than he had when he was in town before, while Harry was still in jail. I walked out to meet him, and that's when he told me that he had his men standin' guard all around the town, with orders to shoot anybody who tried to get out. He said . . ." Webber had to stop for a second. His face was gray and strained, with deep trenches in his cheeks above the bushy white mustache. "He said that he was gonna kill everybody in town and burn Dry Creek to the ground to settle the score for his boy. I told him he was crazy, that he couldn't do such a thing no matter what had happened, but he didn't listen to me. He was like God pronouncin' doom on the Israelites or somethin'."

"But he didn't say when this was going to happen?"

Webber shook his head. "Nope, he just turned his horse around and rode out."

Deborah said, "He wanted to frighten us. It makes his vengeance even better knowing that we're sitting here waiting for him to strike."

Longarm nodded. He knew that Deborah was probably right. Torrance intended to wage a war of nerves before taking his revenge. But he wouldn't wait too long, for fear that the townspeople might somehow get out word of what was going on and ask for help.

"He's out of his head with grief and rage," Deborah

went on. "If he would just stop and think about it, he'd know that he can't hope to get away with an atrocity like the one he's planning."

"When too many folks know a secret, it ain't a secret anymore," commented Longarm, echoing his thoughts of a few moments earlier about the reason for Barney Whitten's suicide. "He'd have to deal with all of his ranch hands knowing what happened. The story would be bound to get out." Another thought occurred to him. "What about Torrance's crew? Will they really be willing to ride in here and murder everybody in town, including the women and kids?"

"Some men will do most anything if the money's good enough," said Webber. "And Cy's got plenty of money. I expect he'd spend every penny he has to his name if that's what it takes to even the score for Harry. And the fellas who ain't willin' to take part in the killin' . . . well, somebody's still got to ride around the town and keep it shut off from the rest o' the world."

Longarm supposed Webber was right. He knew there were plenty of men on the frontier who wouldn't draw the line at murder if the payment was right. He had crossed trails with such hombres more times than he liked to think about.

"All right," he said after a long moment of thought. "You can't just sit here and wait for Torrance to ride in and kill everybody."

"We haven't been sittin' and waitin'. We're gonna put up a fight. I got lookouts posted, and folks are forted up in the buildings with plenty of guns and ammunition."

"But people will still die," said Deborah. "And what will happen when Torrance's men set fire to the buildings, like you know they will? We can either stay inside and roast, or go out to escape the flames and be shot down like dogs." She shook her head. "In the end, we'll all die if we stay here, Frank, and you know it."

"Well, blast it, what else can we do except stay and

fight?" exclaimed Webber. "You heard what Torrance said. Anybody who tries to leave will get shot too."

"What if all of you break out of the settlement at once?" suggested Longarm.

The other two looked at him.

"Get everyone in town either on horseback or in a wagon or buggy," Longarm went on. "How many men does Torrance have working for him?"

"It's a big spread," replied Webber. "He's got probably fifty or sixty hands, maybe more."

"So they're bound to be stretched pretty thin if they have the whole town surrounded. You could bust through the line."

"Torrance would come after us. Then we'd have a runnin' fight on our hands, and we'd be out in the open with no cover at all."

Webber had a point, thought Longarm. An escape attempt might be just trading one danger for another.

Deborah said, "Besides, we'd have to leave almost everything behind. Our homes, our businesses, our possessions . . . all of that would be lost when Torrance put the town to the torch. And that's exactly what he'd do, Marshal. Make no mistake about that."

Longarm didn't doubt it. Some of the citizens wouldn't be willing to leave under those conditions. They would prefer to stay and fight, even if they were doomed to lose. Longarm understood that feeling and even sympathized with it. He didn't have much give-up in him either.

"All right then," he said with a solemn nod. "The way I see it, there's only one thing left to try. Somebody's got to get to Torrance and try to talk some sense into his head."

"Can't be done," said Webber. "Anyway, who'd be a big enough fool to try a stunt like that?"

Longarm smiled without humor and said, "I figured on nominating myself."

Chapter 10

Webber and Deborah both stared at him in disbelief for several seconds before the local lawman said, "That won't do nothin' except get you killed a mite quicker, Marshal."

"Maybe not," said Longarm. "Once Torrance hears that a federal lawman knows what he's up to, maybe he'll realize what a crazy idea it is and leave you folks alone."

"Or maybe he'll just go ahead and kill you, like Marshal Webber said," Deborah objected.

Longarm shrugged. "Any chance is better than nothing."

Webber frowned and pulled at his chin. "Yeah . . ." he said. "Maybe. I don't see how it could make things any worse." He glanced at the front window of the café. "The sun'll be down in another hour. Better wait until after dark. You'd have a better chance of gettin' past Torrance's men then."

Longarm nodded. "You'll have to tell me how to find Torrance's ranch."

"I can do that."

Deborah looked back and forth between Longarm and Webber and then shook her head. "I still think it's a bad idea," she said, "but I can see that you won't be talked out of it. Can I get you another cup of coffee before you go?"

This time when Longarm smiled, the expression was genuine. "I'd like that just fine, ma'am," he said as he extended his empty cup.

Marshal Webber added, "We're gonna need a couple of meals for the prisoners too, Deborah."

She nodded. "I'll put some trays together."

Webber watched her with frank admiration in his eyes as she got up and went into the kitchen. "That there is a fine woman," he said, pitching his voice quietly enough so that Deborah wouldn't hear him. "Damn shame all the trouble she's had in her life."

"What trouble is that?" asked Longarm.

"Her husband was killed in an accident a couple of years ago. Jim Kane was our blacksmith. Horse went loco while he was tryin' to shoe it and kicked him in the head. He lingered for a couple of days before passin' on."

Longarm shook his head. "That's a damned shame."

"Sure as hell was. Deborah bore up under it, though. I reckon she felt she had to, on account of her little girl and all. Wasn't long after Jim died that Sarah Gilley and her folks came to Dry Creek too, and Deborah took on a lot of the responsibility for takin' care of Sarah after the fever took her ma and pa. And she opened up this café too, so she'd have a way of makin' a livin'."

"Sounds to me like she was trying to stay busy all the time," said Longarm. "Busy enough so that losing her husband didn't hurt quite so much maybe."

Webber shrugged. "You might have somethin' there. All I know for sure is that she's a fine woman."

"You married, Marshal?" asked Longarm.

"Huh? No, I ain't married. What're you . . . oh, hell, you don't think that me an' Deborah . . . ?" Webber gave an emphatic shake of his head. "I'm purdee near old enough to be her grandpa! Well, her pa anyway. No maybe about that. I admire the hell out of her, but I ain't got no designs on her or nothin' like that."

Longarm nodded. "I was just curious, Marshal. It doesn't matter to me one way or the other. All I'm worried about now is taking care of my prisoners and finding a way to head off the trouble that's about to descend on this town."

"Anything you can do, I'll be much obliged for." Webber drained the rest of his coffee, which had grown cold in the cup. He leaned back in his chair, looked reflective, and went on. "I reckon I shouldn't have told you what happened to Harry Torrance. If Cy don't kill me, you're liable to arrest me and all the others who were in on the hangin'."

"I don't approve of lynching," said Longarm, "but that's a matter for the county sheriff. He'll hear about it sooner or later, and then you'll have to deal with him."

Webber sighed. "I know. And I'll take whatever I've got comin' to me. The responsibility is mine, more'n it is the fellas who actually strung Harry up. I should've stopped 'em." His big, gnarled hands clenched into fists again. "I just couldn't stop thinkin' about how poor Sarah looked and how much pain she must've gone through before she died. I couldn't let Harry get away with doin' that."

Longarm didn't say anything, and he was saved from the necessity of doing so by Deborah Kane's return. She put a fresh cup of coffee on the table in front of him and said, "I'll have those trays ready for the prisoners in a few minutes. Who are they anyway?"

"You remember a couple named Bramlett?" asked Webber. "Had a homestead several miles south o' here?"

Deborah nodded. "I think so. The woman has fair hair and is rather pretty?"

"That's right," Longarm said. "She killed her husband. An outlaw I've been chasing stopped at their place, and Mrs. Bramlett wanted to run off with him to San Francisco. So she shot Bramlett in the back."

"That's terrible! I can't imagine such a thing."

Longarm recalled what Webber had told him about how Deborah Kane had lost her husband to a tragic accident. Deborah probably would have done almost anything to save Jim Kane's life, while Mollie Bramlett had cold-bloodedly murdered her spouse on a whim.

Folks were funny, but not so that Longarm felt much like laughing at moments like this.

"I've got that owlhoot locked up down in my jail cell," explained Webber, "and Miz Bramlett is in one of the rooms at the hotel. I'll turn her over to the sheriff, assumin' we make it through this business with Cy Torrance."

"And I'll be taking Tom Rankin back to Denver with me," Longarm added.

Deborah nodded. "All three of you should have ridden some other direction," she said. "Then you wouldn't be trapped here."

"Too late for that now," said Longarm.

"Yes. I'll get those trays."

She returned from the kitchen a few minutes later with two trays, each containing a plate covered by a clean cloth. Longarm and Webber took them, and the local lawman said, "The town will pay you for these meals, Deborah."

She smiled. "Again, assuming we all survive."

"Well, yeah."

Longarm put a double eagle on the table and gave the woman a polite nod. "Hope I'll see you again, ma'am. In the meantime, I'm obliged to you for your hospitality."

Deborah picked up the coin. "This is a lot more than what you owe me for your supper, Marshal Long."

"Well, maybe I'll eat a few more meals here before I go. I hope so anyway."

"And if we're all dead by morning, what do a few dollars matter?"

"Better go easy on that optimism, ma'am," Longarm told her with a grin. "You might hurt yourself."

For a second, she looked like she was going to get angry with him, but then she burst out in a laugh. "You're right," she said as she slipped the double eagle in the pocket of her apron. "There's no point in giving up, is there?"

"Not hardly," said Longarm.

He and Webber left the café. They went to the Plaza Hotel first. Webber held both trays while Longarm unlocked the door to Room Seven. He had his hand on the butt of his Colt as he swung the door open and said, "Got your supper here, ma'am."

Mollie Bramlett didn't reply. Longarm had a bad moment when he wondered if she might have harmed herself, but when he stepped into the room he saw her sitting on the edge of the bed, staring at the wall. Her head turned a little and her eyes flicked toward him for a second, but that was the only sign she gave that she knew he was there.

Webber set one of the trays on the table next to the bed. "There you go, ma'am," he said. "Don't worry about the tray. I'll get it in the mornin' when I bring your breakfast up to you."

Mollie still didn't acknowledge them. The two men backed out of the room, and Longarm relocked the door.

"Gal's a mite spooky," Webber commented as they went downstairs.

"She's had her whole life turned upside down today," said Longarm. "A lot of it is her own fault, but even so it's enough to throw a person off stride."

They crossed the street to the jail after telling Everett and the other men in the lobby that there was no sign of Torrance and his men, as far as they knew. The waiting game continued.

Tom Rankin jumped up from the bunk in the cell and gripped the bars hard as soon as Longarm and Webber came into the marshal's office. "Damn it," said the outlaw, "you've gotta let me out of here, Long! I've been thinkin' about it, and you've got no right to keep me locked up so some crazy rancher can kill me along with everybody else in town!"

"Maybe you should've thought about that before you held up those trains and stagecoaches and killed the lawman down south of here," Longarm pointed out.

"How the hell could I have known how it would all turn out?"

"You ain't helpin' your case, old son. Now, you want some supper or not?"

In a sullen, grudging voice, Rankin said, "Yeah, yeah, I'm hungry. I'll take the food."

The barred door had a slot for trays. Webber passed it through. Rankin took it, went back to the bunk, sat down, and began to eat, gnawing hungrily on a cold chicken leg.

Longarm and Webber stepped out onto the porch. Longarm took a cheroot from his shirt pocket and examined it in the fading light. It was a mite bent from the wrestling he had done with Rankin the night before, but he figured it was better than nothing. He clamped his teeth on one end of the cheroot, snapped a lucifer to life with an iron-hard thumbnail, and held the flame to the other end.

Webber took out a pipe and a pouch of tobacco and soon had it going. As clouds of smoke wreathed his head, he said, "I'll be goin' on my evening rounds soon. Might as well stay in the habit, even though I may never do it again. You want to come with me, Marshal?"

"No, I think I'll walk down to the stable and see about getting a fresh mount."

"You may need it if you try to get out of here and reach Torrance's ranch. Tell Eph Bridges I said to give you the best horse he's got."

"I'll do that." Longarm lifted a hand in farewell. "See you later, Marshal."

He untied his mount, Rankin's horse, and the Bramlett mule from the hitch rail in front of the marshal's office and led the animals down the street toward the livery stable he had spotted earlier. As he walked past the café, he noted that the lamps had been blown out and the sign in the window was turned around so that it read CLOSED. He supposed that Deborah Kane had decided against staying open this evening after all.

Eph Bridges was a short, round, mostly bald man with the face of a cherub and the high-pitched voice of a child. Like everybody else in Dry Creek, he was waiting nervously to see what Cy Torrance was going to do. But when Longarm introduced himself and explained what he was going to do, Bridges led out a black gelding with white stockings and a white blaze.

"This is the best horse I've got, Marshal, just like Frank said. You're welcome to slap your saddle on him, and I wish you the best of luck in your errand."

"You know Cy Torrance pretty well?" asked Longarm.

Bridges nodded. "I've known him for years. I used to have a little spread in these parts, next to Cy's Rocking T. When I got a little older, I decided to sell it to him and get out while I could. I knew he had his eye on the place and wanted to add it to his holdings. He sometimes made things tough on the smaller ranchers until they sold out to him at his price. Cy Torrance is the sort of man who gets what he wants, no matter who else gets hurt."

"Then you think he's capable of doing what he's threatened to do?"

"I think Cy Torrance is capable of damn near anything, Marshal."

Longarm didn't like the sound of that, but it was the sort of answer he'd been expecting. He thanked Eph Bridges and led the blaze-faced gelding back along the street. The sun was down now and shadows were gathering. Longarm intended to stop at the jail one more time and get directions to Torrance's ranch from Marshal Webber.

Before he could get there, though, he had to pass the café again, and this time as he did so, the door opened, taking him by surprise since the place was still dark. As he turned toward it, Deborah Kane appeared in the doorway, visible in the faint light, and said, "Marshal Long, could you come in here, please?"

Longarm looped the reins around the hitch rack in front of the café and stepped up onto the porch. "I suppose so, ma'am," he said. He took his hat off as he followed her into the building. Deborah turned and closed the door behind him. The curtains were pulled over the windows, but enough faint gray light still came in so that he could see her as she moved in front of him.

"What can I do for you, Mrs. Kane?" he asked with a slight frown as he stood there holding his hat.

She moved closer, reached out, and rested her fingertips on his arm. In a voice that sounded as if she were having trouble getting the words out, she said, "You can make love to me, Marshal Long."

Chapter 11

Longarm's frown deepened. "I don't know if that's a good idea, ma'am," he said. "The little girl . . ."

"I've sent Lucy to spend the evening at a friend's house. They're children. They . . . they don't really understand what's going on. They know there may be some trouble, but that's all. It'll be good for them to spend some time together, playing and laughing."

"And you want to spend that time—"

Her fingers tightened on his arm. "Do you want me to say it?" she asked in a voice that trembled a little with emotion. "I want to feel a man inside me again. I want to feel a man's weight on top of me. I want that heat, that release . . . I was married for almost ten years, Marshal, but since my husband . . . died . . . I haven't . . . not even once . . ."

Longarm dropped his hat on one of the tables and reached up to touch her shoulder. "It's all right," he said. "I reckon I understand. I ain't so sure it's a good idea, though."

She stiffened. "Why not?"

"You never even laid eyes on me until an hour or so ago. I know you want to feel close to somebody again, but there ought to be somebody in this town who knows you who'd be a better choice for that."

A soft laugh came from her. "You think I haven't thought about it before now? This isn't just because . . . because we may all be dead before morning. I never set out to be lonely the rest of my life. I know Jim wouldn't have wanted that. But to tell you the truth, there's *not* another man in this town who . . . who touches something in me the way you did when you first walked in here with Frank Webber. I haven't felt this way since my husband died. The situation with Cy Torrance just makes things a bit more . . . urgent, I guess you'd say."

Longarm rested both hands on her shoulders now. She moved closer to him and slipped her arms around his waist. Their bodies touched, but only tentatively.

"Don't make me beg, Marshal Long," said Deborah. "You'll make me feel like a . . . a trollop."

"You ain't hardly that, ma'am." He bent and brushed his lips over hers. "And under the circumstances, I reckon you'd better start calling me Custis."

"Only if you stop calling me ma'am," she said. Then she came up on her toes and crushed her mouth against his in an urgent, passionate kiss that sent heat searing through Longarm.

He responded with an equal intensity. His first thought, other than the worry that Deborah was making an impulsive, hasty decision that she might regret later, was that he didn't have time for this because he was on his way to try to escape from the cordon Torrance had thrown around the town, then find the rancher and try to talk some sense into his head. But it would actually be better if he waited for a while longer before attempting to leave Dry Creek, he realized, because then it would be darker and he would stand a better chance of slipping past Torrance's trigger-happy cowboys.

So, given all that—and given the fact that he always

liked to oblige a lady whenever possible—he thought he could afford to spend a little time with Deborah Kane.

He probed her lips with his tongue, and they parted eagerly. Her hands clutched at his back through his shirt as their tongues met and engaged in a hot, wet, sensuous dance. Longarm moved his right hand down from her left shoulder to her left breast. She still wore the gingham dress and the white apron, but even through those intervening layers of cloth, he could feel her nipple hardening against his palm as he cupped the firm globe of female flesh. He ran his thumb over it, and the caress made it poke out even more.

Deborah moved her hands from his back to the front of his butternut shirt. Her fingers worked to unfasten the buttons. She seemed to have a little trouble with them because her hands were trembling. Finally, she had several buttons undone and slid her hands inside to feel his broad, muscular chest that was matted with dark brown hair.

As they continued to kiss, Longarm reached behind her to massage the small of her back. That made her push her pelvis forward against his groin. She gasped against his lips as she ground herself on the hard pole inside his denim trousers.

Longarm pulled the back of her dress up, and found to his surprise that she was naked underneath it. She must have removed her undergarments before she even summoned him in here. He splayed his hands over the bare cheeks of her rump, kneading and caressing them. She broke the kiss at last and rested her head on his chest, still quivering from the depth of the feelings going through her.

Longarm was pretty aroused too, and his shaft was so hard it was becoming a mite uncomfortable in the close confines of his trousers. He was glad when Deborah reached down to unfasten the buttons of his fly and free the long, thick organ. As it jutted out in front of his groin, she wrapped both hands around it and breathed, "Oh, my God.

It's been so long, Custis, so long since I held a man . . . and there's so much of you! I can't . . . I can't possibly take it all in . . ." Suddenly, she giggled like a girl. "But I sure intend to try!"

Longarm chuckled. "That's the spirit. Do we need to, uh, go back to your house where there's a bed?"

"There's a bunk in the storeroom, next to the kitchen," she said with a shake of her head. "I sometimes lie down there to rest in the middle of the day, between dinner and supper. We can put it to even better use now."

She took his hand, turned, and led him through the kitchen to the storeroom. Longarm lit a match and held the flame to the wick of a small lantern that Deborah told him was sitting on a shelf in the room. Even though the flickering glow it gave off was faint, Longarm was grateful for it, because it provided enough light for him to see the graceful, sensuous lines of her body as she pulled her clothes off. Her erect, dark brown nipples weren't overly large, but they stuck out a good half an inch as they crowned each breast. Her legs were good, the thighs flowing sleekly into the curves of her hips, and between them was a thick triangle of dark hair. She caught hold of Longarm's right hand with both of hers and brought it to her groin, where she pressed it hard against the mound that was covered by that fine-spun hair.

"That feels *so* good," she whispered.

Longarm rotated the ball of his hand where it rested on her mound. That caused Deborah to close her eyes and make little noises of pleasure. Her hips jerked as he reached down with his middle finger and found the sensitive bud of flesh at the top of her already drenched opening.

She tugged at his shirt. "Get the rest of those clothes off!" she urged with a note of desperation creeping into her voice.

Longarm complied, shucking his duds as quickly as he could while Deborah lay back on the blanket-covered bunk. He hoped it was sturdy enough to support both of them.

Might cause a real problem if it collapsed under them.

He was willing to risk it, though. When he was naked, Deborah sat up on the edge of the bunk and reached out to grasp his shaft again. She leaned forward and rubbed the head against her cheek. She moved her face around, caressing him with her nose, her chin, her forehead. Moisture was already leaking from the slit on the end, and it left a trail of heat on her skin.

"This is the most beautiful thing I've ever seen," she said. "Later, if there's time, I want . . . I don't know if I can say it, it's too shameful." But she rushed on anyway. "I want to taste it, Custis."

Longarm stroked her hair and smiled down at her. "I reckon that could be arranged."

"Right now, though . . . I want you inside me!"

She lay back again and opened herself to him, spreading her thighs wide in invitation. The lantern light gleamed on the lips of her femininity. Longarm moved to mount her, kneeling between her legs and bringing the head of his shaft to her opening. She grasped his hips as he poised above her.

Then he drove down and in, opening her with a powerful thrust and sheathing himself inside her. She was so wet that he went in easily at first, but then he could tell that she had never before had a cock as big as his in her. Her eyes opened wide as her sex stretched to accommodate him.

"I . . . I've never been so full!" she gasped. "Oh, Custis!"

She brought her knees up and wrapped her legs around his hips as he began to pump in and out of her. As he bent down to kiss her, she put her arms around his neck and held him with surprising strength, the strength of a woman being made love to passionately and skillfully and enjoying every second of it. Her hips bucked as she met his thrusts with her own.

Given the amount of time that had passed since the last time Deborah had had a man, Longarm didn't expect her

71

climax to be long in arriving. Sure enough, it boiled up after only a few moments. She jerked and spasmed underneath him and cried out in ecstasy. He eased off and let her enjoy it, keeping his shaft buried within her but not moving much as shudders of delight rolled through her.

Only when the most intense moment seemed to be past did he start thrusting into her again, slowly but powerfully. She had closed her eyes as her culmination swept over her, but now she opened them again and stared up at him.

"Custis . . . ?"

"Just enjoy it," he told her, then kissed her forehead. "I can keep going awhile longer."

"Oh. Oh!" Her arousal was already starting to build back up again.

Longarm wanted this to be as good for Deborah as it possibly could, but even he had his limits. After she had come a second time, he began pounding harder and faster into her. She got caught up in the rhythm, and as he felt his own culmination surging through him, no longer to be denied, she spasmed again. Longarm drove into her one final time, delving deeper than ever before, and stayed there as his throbbing shaft exploded. His juices emptied into her, filling her with heat so fierce that both of them basked in it for long moments.

Finally, though, Longarm pushed himself up so that his weight wasn't crushing her to the bunk. Deborah clutched at him and said, "Custis, surely you don't have to go so soon . . ."

"I wish I didn't," Longarm told her. "I wouldn't like anything more than to stay right here with you all night."

"But you have a job to do, and I have a little girl." Deborah's voice had a bittersweet twist to it. "And this moment, as nice as it was, was just a moment, something that with luck we can both remember . . . You *will* remember me, won't you?"

Longarm leaned down and kissed her again. "I reckon you can count on that," he said in a husky whisper.

He might have said more, and she might have tempted him to stay a little longer, but at that moment he heard a sound from outside, and even though he didn't realize what it was at first, his instincts warned him that something was wrong.

Then he recognized the sound as someone yelling in alarm.

"Custis, what is it?" exclaimed Deborah as Longarm rolled off the bunk and stood up. He grabbed his clothes and began pulling them on as fast as he could. Then Deborah heard the shouting too, and pressed a hand to her mouth. "Oh, my God!" she said around it. "It's started!"

"Maybe not," Longarm said as he pulled his boots on and reached for his gunbelt. As he belted the cross-draw rig around his waist, he went on. "I haven't heard any shots, and if Torrance and his men were attacking the town, there'd be a bigger ruckus."

"Then what is it?"

He shook his head. "I don't know, but I intend to find out."

He snatched up his hat and headed for the door. As he opened it, Deborah leaped from the bunk and wrapped the blanket around her nakedness. "I'm coming with you!"

Longarm shook his head. "Stay here," he snapped, and his tone of command brooked no argument. "Actually, what you'd better do is get dressed and go find Lucy."

"Oh, Lord, Lucy! You're right." She dropped the blanket and plucked her dress from the floor where she had dropped it in her haste to make love with Longarm. As he went out the door, she called after him, "Be careful, Custis!"

Longarm hurried through the kitchen and the front room of the café. As he emerged on the street, he realized that several people were shouting now, calling questions back and forth. The sounds came from somewhere along the creek, behind the buildings on the other side of the street. Longarm left the horse he'd gotten at the livery stable where it was tied and ran toward the troubling sounds.

As he emerged at the back of a narrow alley between two buildings, he spotted a cluster of people at the edge of the streambed. They seemed to be agitated about something, but he couldn't tell what it was. The shadows cast by the cottonwoods along the bank were too thick. The moon had not yet risen, but the myriad stars provided quite a bit of light. It just didn't reach under the trees.

Somebody struck a match and lit a lantern just as Longarm trotted up to the group, though, and as the yellow glow grew brighter, it illuminated an unexpected and horrifying scene. The nearest tree wasn't the one where Harry Torrance had been strung up, but one of its branches had a hangrope tied to it anyway. Unlike the other, this noose hadn't been cut off. It was still at the end of the rope.

And inside it was the neck of the liveryman, Eph Bridges. The noose was so tight that the rope dug into the flesh of the man's neck. Fat bulged around it.

Bridges's eyes bulged even more, and so did his tongue. There was a bloody contusion on his forehead. He hung a good two feet off the ground, swaying back and forth ever so slightly, and there was no doubt whatsoever that he was dead.

Chapter 12

One of the men in the group turned to glance at Longarm, then exclaimed, "Hey, who are you?" He started to lift the rifle he carried. "By God, if you're one of Torrance's men, mister—"

"Take it easy, Yates," said one of the other men. Longarm recognized him as Everett, the proprietor of the Plaza Hotel. "That's the federal marshal I was telling you about earlier. Frank Webber can vouch for him."

That lessened the air of tension among the men, but not by much. Longarm nodded toward the hanging corpse and asked, "Who found him?"

"I did," replied one of the men in a voice roughened by shock. "I was coming along here to relieve one of the guards on the other side of the creek when I saw poor Eph hangin' there. I let out a yell and ran back to Main Street to get help."

"Did you recognize him when you saw him?"

The man shook his head. "No, not really. To tell you the truth . . ." He stopped and rubbed his beard-stubbled jaw for a second before continuing. "To tell you the truth, at first I thought it was . . . was Harry Torrance, come back from the dead. Then I realized this wasn't the tree where

75

Harry was—" His voice was choked off by the memory, as surely as if that hangrope had been around *his* neck, instead of Bridges's.

Heavy footsteps sounded in the darkness as another man hurried up to join the group. "What in blazes is goin' on here?" asked Marshal Frank Webber. Then he looked up, saw Eph Bridges, and exclaimed, "Good Lord!"

"Who could've done such a thing, Marshal?" asked one of the townsmen.

Webber shook his head. "I don't know. Poor ol' Eph never hurt anybody in his whole life—" Webber stopped short, then made a curt gesture toward the body and ordered, "Somebody cut him down from there."

"Hold on," said Longarm. He took the lantern from the man holding it and approached the hanged man. Lifting the lantern so that its light washed over Bridges's body and the hangrope and the ground underneath the corpse, Longarm studied everything for several minutes, memorizing the scene as best he could in case anything about it should prove later to be important.

Finally, he lowered the lantern and gave it back to the man who had brought it out here. "Go ahead," he said to the others. "You got an undertaker in Dry Creek?"

"Yeah," said Webber. "Take him to Thad Cooley's place, boys."

One of the men climbed into the tree and cut the rope with a barlow knife while the others gathered underneath Bridges's body to catch hold of it and lower it to the ground. Then several of the men picked up the corpse and carried it off toward Dry Creek's main street. The rest of the group followed, but Longarm motioned for Webber to hang back with him.

When the others were far enough away not to overhear, Longarm asked the local lawman, "Was Bridges one of the men who strung up Harry Torrance?"

Shadows masked Webber's face, but his voice was grim

as he replied, "He sure as hell was. You reckon Cy's decided to hang the fellas who were involved, instead of wipin' out the whole town?"

"Maybe. Or maybe this is just one more way for him to make people suffer for a while before he attacks."

"That cold-blooded bastard," grated Webber.

"Some French hombre once wrote that revenge is a dish best served cold," said Longarm. "I reckon maybe Torrance has decided that taking his time is better than attacking right away. That's all right. Gives me more time to try to get to him."

"He's murdered Eph Bridges now," Webber pointed out, "or had some of his men do it anyway. Jess Garth or some of those hard cases who ride for the Rocking T must've snuck into town, taken poor Eph out of the stable, and brought him down here to string him up. With a murder charge hangin' over his head, you won't be able to talk sense into Torrance and get him to give up his crazy ideas."

"Maybe not," admitted Longarm. "But there might be something else I can do."

Webber asked, "What the hell you got in mind, Marshal?"

Longarm dodged the question. "Let me think about it. There's got to be a way to salvage this situation, and waiting for Torrance and his men to ride in shooting isn't it."

"All right, but if there's anything I can do to help . . ."

"I'll let you know, Marshal," Longarm promised.

They walked back to the street, and as they passed through the alley between buildings, Longarm thought about everything that had happened. He had left Eph Bridges at the stable only a short time earlier. He had been in the café with Deborah Kane for only about half an hour before hearing the shouts from the man who had discovered the liveryman's body.

That meant whoever had killed Bridges had done it quickly. Of course, Longarm asked himself, how long

77

would it take to grab an old man, drag him down to the creek, throw a rope over a limb, and drag him off the ground by his neck?

Longarm's jaw tightened as he thought about the way Bridges had died. Unlike falling through the trapdoor of a gallows, there had been no short, sharp snap to break his neck at the end of the drop. Instead, Bridges had strangled to death slowly, passing what had probably been a terrifying, agonizing several minutes before losing consciousness and then letting death claim him.

A cold dish indeed.

Webber had posted men around the settlement to watch for any signs of an attack by Torrance's men, but they were probably spread out quite a bit. It was possible that some of the Rocking T riders had slipped through the cordon, as Webber suggested, and murdered Eph Bridges before sneaking out of town again. Nothing about the scene of the hanging indicated otherwise. Longarm had studied the ground, looking for tracks, but the group of townsmen had milled around so much that it was impossible to pick out any distinctive marks from the welter of footprints.

"So you're still ridin' out to Torrance's spread?" asked Webber just before they reached the street.

Longarm nodded. "That's right, if you'll tell me how to find it. I want to take a look around the place anyway." A vague plan was beginning to form in his head, but he would have to visit the Rocking T to see whether or not it would stand a chance of working.

Webber explained that Torrance's ranch was located north of the settlement and told him which trail to take, then added, "Seems a mite like a fool's errand to me now, but I guess that's up to you, Marshal. At least you've got that blaze-faced gelding to ride. That's a good horse, plenty of speed and sand."

"Looked like it to me too," agreed Longarm. "So long,

Marshal." He left the alley and walked over to the hitch rack where the gelding waited, and untied the reins.

Longarm turned the horse and heeled it into a trot. As he rode past the darkened café, he saw Deborah Kane and her daughter walking along the street toward it. Deborah must have realized by now that Torrance wasn't attacking the town after all, but she had fetched Lucy from her friend's house anyway. As Longarm passed them, he gave the brim of his flat-crowned, snuff brown Stetson a polite tug and said, "Evening, ladies."

"Good evening, Marshal," said Deborah, as if she hadn't been panting and climaxing underneath him less than a half hour earlier.

"Hello, Marshal," Lucy piped up. "Where are you going this late? It's bedtime."

Longarm reined in and said, "I reckon you're right, Miss Lucy, but sometimes a fella has to keep working even though there's nothing he'd like better than to slip into a warm, comfortable bed somewhere."

"Yes, that does sound nice, doesn't it?" said Deborah. "Wherever you're going, be careful, Marshal Long. We'll keep you in our thoughts and prayers. Won't we, Lucy?"

"Sure," said the little girl as she smiled up at Longarm. She echoed her mother. "Be careful, Marshal."

Longarm didn't tell her that he intended to. He just smiled and nodded again, then lifted the reins, clucked to the blaze-faced gelding, and got moving. He didn't look back, but he could feel Deborah and Lucy watching him and hoped that he wasn't leaving Dry Creek for the last time.

Chapter 13

Once he had forded the shallow creek and put the settlement behind him, Longarm pulled the horse back to a
walk. He wanted to move across the prairie as quietly as he
could, so as not to alert Torrance's men that someone was
trying to get out of town. A silvery glow in the eastern sky
told him that the moon would be coming up soon. He had
intended to leave earlier, but the interlude with Deborah
Kane and then the discovery of Eph Bridges's body had
delayed him. In Deborah's case, Longarm didn't mind. The
time he had spent with her had been worth it. He would
have just as soon that Bridges hadn't been murdered. He
had liked the garrulous little liveryman, even though he
knew that Bridges had been part of the group that lynched
Harry Torrance.

Longarm had mixed emotions about that hanging. He
had been known to bend the law himself on occasion in order to insure that justice was done, and as far as the citizens
of Dry Creek had known, Harry was guilty of a heinous
crime, raping and murdering a beautiful young woman
who'd had the mind of a child. Knowing Cy Torrance the
way they did, knowing how arrogant and high-handed he
was and that he had a pack of gun-handy hard cases working

for him, it was reasonable to assume that Torrance would never let his son be executed and probably wouldn't even allow him to come to trial.

To the citizens of Dry Creek, it had seemed like all they were doing was carrying out justice.

The only problem with that idea was that Harry Torrance hadn't been guilty after all. If Barney Whitten was to be believed—and it was hard to doubt the word of a man who was about to die by his own hand—Harry hadn't touched Sarah Gilley. He had died for no good reason at all.

It was a tragic situation all the way around, thought Longarm, but if Cy Torrance was allowed to go through with his plan for a terrible vengeance, things would just get worse. Dozens of innocent people would die. Longarm had to prevent that if he could. If Torrance wasn't completely consumed by hatred, maybe Longarm could make him realize that wiping out Dry Creek wasn't going to bring Harry back.

But the only way to do that would be to get a chance to talk to Torrance alone, and that probably meant getting him away from the ranch somehow.

First things first, Longarm reminded himself. He had to get away from Dry Creek without being killed or captured by Torrance's patrols. With a steady swishing sound of the horse's legs moving through the buffalo grass, Longarm headed northward toward the Rocking T.

The lights of the settlement were still visible in the distance behind Longarm when he heard the thudding of hoofbeats. As the riders approached, he reined in and dismounted, then stood beside the gelding's head, ready to clamp his hand over the animal's nose if the gelding tried to call out to the other horses. If Torrance's gunnies came close enough, they would probably spot him anyway, since he and the horse would form a darker patch against the lighter background of the prairie. In that case, he would have to leap back into the saddle, and the deadly race would be on.

But the men moved on past, a couple of hundred yards away. Longarm saw them in the starlight, but none of them appeared to notice him. He waited until they were out of sight and earshot before he mounted up and rode on.

He didn't believe it was going to be that easy to get past Torrance's men, and ten or fifteen minutes later, that hunch was proved right. The prairie wasn't completely flat, and as he passed a slight rise to his left, a couple of riders suddenly came over the top of it and moved to intercept him. "Hold it right there, mister!" one of them yelled.

Longarm didn't wait. He knew there was no point in trying to talk his way out of this. Instead, he jammed the heels of his boots into the gelding's flanks and sent the horse lunging forward into a gallop.

The two riders shouted angrily and spurred after him. Colt flame bloomed in the darkness as they swept down the shallow hill. Longarm heard bullets whistling over his head as he bent forward over the gelding's neck and urged it on to a faster pace. Since there were only two men, he thought about making a stand, but if he stopped to fight this pair of gunmen, the sound of the shots would draw more of Torrance's men and Longarm would be overwhelmingly outnumbered in no time.

What was it that fella Francis Marion had said back in Revolutionary War times about running away and living to fight another day? Made perfect sense to Longarm at this moment, so he got as much speed as he could out of the blaze-faced gelding.

Six-guns continued to pop and bang behind him. As Longarm galloped across the plains, he hoped that the gelding wouldn't step in some prairie-dog hole that went unseen until it was too late. He wasn't too worried about a bullet finding either of them. The range was long for handguns, and it would be pure bad luck if he or the horse got hit.

Of course, bad luck wasn't unheard of . . .

The moon had crept above the horizon by now, and its silvery glow suddenly illuminated a dark line across the ground in front of Longarm and the racing horse. For a second or two, Longarm couldn't tell what it was, but then as a chill went through him, he realized that his mount was bearing down swiftly on a dry wash that cut across the plains. There was no telling how far it extended in both directions, and if he tried to go around it, Torrance's men would catch him, sure as Hades. The same thing would happen if he slowed down to search for a place where the wash's banks were caved in and he could get across.

No, there were only two real choices, thought Longarm: turn and fight—or keep going.

Webber had said that the horse had plenty of sand. Longarm figured he was about to find out if that was true.

"Trail, you blaze-faced bastard, trail!" he called to the gelding as he slashed the reins back and forth. The wind tugged at his hat, which was held on only by its chin strap. A glance over his shoulder told Longarm that the pursuers hadn't closed in any on him. If anything, they had fallen back a little, making their handguns even less effective. If his horse could make it to the other side of that wash, he had no doubt that he could leave Torrance's men far behind.

But if the horse couldn't make it and came crashing back to earth too soon, Longarm knew that he would probably die in a broken, mangled heap on the bottom of that gully.

"You can do it, old son," he said with a grin on his face. "You can do it!"

As if the horse understood the words, it surged forward, stretching out and running even faster.

The wash seemed to come up in the blink of an eye. Longarm leaned as far forward as he could and loosened his grip on the reins, letting the horse have its head. The gelding never slowed. As the wash opened up before it, the horse's muscles propelled it into the air, soaring up and up and over the empty space yawning beneath it. The wash wasn't more than a dozen feet deep, but it was a good twenty feet wide.

The couple of heartbeats that it took to cover that twenty feet were two of the longest seconds in Longarm's life.

Then the gelding's front hooves slammed down on the far side of the wash and caught hold and carried it forward, and in the blink of an eye the galloping hoofbeats were drumming across the plains again as the wash fell behind them.

Longarm remembered to breathe again a few seconds later.

The guns fell silent behind him, and when he looked back, he couldn't see the pursuers anymore. Just as he had expected, they had given up the chase when they came to the gully, not being brave enough—or foolhardy enough, however you wanted to look at it—to attempt the sort of leap the gelding had made. Torrance might be angry that they had allowed someone to escape from Dry Creek, but they weren't willing to risk a jump like that.

Longarm pulled the horse back to a trot. The shots would draw attention, but he hoped he could reach the Rocking T before a search for him could be organized. That hope strengthened a few minutes later when he came to the trail Frank Webber had mentioned. It was a fairly well-defined wagon road, and Longarm knew that it would lead him right to Torrance's ranch.

Less than half an hour later, he spotted lights in the distance. He figured they came from the ranch house or some of the other buildings. Torrance had a large, successful spread and a big crew. His headquarters probably included a bunkhouse, several barns and corrals, a cookshack, a smokehouse, maybe a separate cabin for the foreman or quarters for married ranch hands, a blacksmith shop, and a storage building or two. The Rocking T wouldn't be any little greasy-sack outfit.

Longarm veered off the trail as he approached. He couldn't just ride in openly and demand to see Torrance. He wanted to get the lay of the land first and figure out a way he could approach Torrance without having to go through a dozen of the cattleman's gun throwers.

Circling to the west, Longarm continued to close in on the scattered lights. When he was about five hundred yards away, he reined the gelding to a halt, swung down from the saddle, and patted the horse on the shoulder.

"Stay here, old son," he said as he let the reins trail to the ground. "I'll be back after a while."

He hoped he would be able to keep that promise, even though he was just making it to a horse.

From there, he approached the Rocking T's headquarters on foot, moving in slowly and carefully toward the buildings. In the moonlight, he could make out the ranch house itself, a big two-story structure. It must have cost a pretty penny to have the lumber to build it freighted in. Longarm would have been willing to bet that when Cy Torrance started the ranch, the original headquarters had been a sod shack. The fact that all the buildings appeared to be constructed from thick planks told Longarm that Torrance was a wealthy man.

Money couldn't bring his son back, though. In this case, all money could buy was vengeance.

Even though lights were still burning in several of the buildings, the hour was late enough so that nobody was moving around the ranch. Keeping to the shadows as much as possible, Longarm crept toward the big house. A lighted window on the first floor drew his attention.

He had thought that Torrance might have guards posted, but so far he hadn't seen any sign of that. Could be that Torrance felt so secure here in the middle of his spread that he didn't feel any need for such precautions. Whatever the reason, Longarm was grateful that he hadn't had to dodge any sentries on his way in.

When he reached the lighted window that was his destination, he crouched beside it, took off his hat, and edged his head past the window frame so he could peer through the glass. Curtains were drawn over the window inside, but they were thin enough so that he could see through them. He was looking into a room that was part office, part study, part library. It was dominated by a big rolltop desk, and a man sat at that desk, staring moodily into space, fingers curled around a squat crystal glass that contained several inches of amber liquid. As Longarm watched, the man picked up the glass, threw back the drink, then refilled it from a brown bottle that was sitting on the desk.

Longarm's instincts told him he was looking at Cy Torrance. Considering the man's reputation, he was a surprisingly unimpressive physical specimen. Short and slender, he had gray hair and a neatly clipped gray mustache. He slumped in the chair, and considering the fact that the bottle was half empty, Longarm suspected that Torrance had put away the other half tonight. The rancher was seeking solace in the booze, but he wasn't likely to find it.

The window was open a couple of inches. Longarm wondered if he could slide it up far enough for him to climb into the room without making enough noise to alert Torrance. The idea that had come to him earlier continued to intrigue him. If he could get his hands on Torrance and knock the rancher unconscious, then get away from the ranch without anyone knowing, he could take Torrance back to Dry Creek. Torrance's men wouldn't dare attack the settlement if their boss was being held prisoner there. Longarm could force Torrance to call off the siege and then send someone to the county seat for help from the sheriff.

He intended to try that anyway, but the first step was getting into the room where Torrance sat drowning his sorrow in Who-hit-John. Longarm put his hat on and slipped his hands under the window.

But before he could try to open it farther, a deep-throated growl sounded behind him, and as he turned his head he saw a large, shadowy shape leaping toward him, fangs bared.

Chapter 14

Longarm whirled, snatching his hat off his head again as he spun around toward the dog. He shoved his left fist inside the Stetson and thrust it in front of his face, blocking the big dog's fangs as they came at his throat. The sharp teeth cut through the hat and pierced Longarm's hand as the powerful jaws clamped shut, but the hat protected him somewhat. The next instant, the dog's weight slammed into him and knocked him back against the house.

So much for stealth. Unless Torrance was deaf as well as drunk, he had to have heard the thud as the dog rammed Longarm against the wall. The furry varmint was growling and snarling loud enough to wake the dead too. With his plan ruined, all Longarm could do now was try to keep the beast from ripping his throat out.

The dog's weight forced him to the ground. Pinned there, Longarm used the hat to fend off the slashing teeth while he reached across his body with his other hand and palmed out the Colt from the cross-draw rig on his left hip. He reversed the gun, gripping it by the cylinder. His arm rose and fell as he brought the gun butt down hard against the dog's head. The canine skull was a thick one, though, and Longarm had to wallop him again before the dog whimpered, went limp, and rolled off him.

Longarm finished shoving the unconscious dog aside and started to scramble to his feet. As he did so, the window was thrust up behind him and a gun roared. The bullet whipped past Longarm's ear. He could have whirled around and maybe ventilated Torrance, but he didn't want to kill the cattleman. He still hoped that he might be able to head off further violence.

So Longarm flipped the Colt around, caught hold of the butt, and fired, aiming at the window frame to drive Torrance back. The slug chewed splinters from the wood. Torrance yelled in pain and disappeared, just as Longarm hoped would happen. Now he had a few seconds to try to get away.

That respite was even shorter than he hoped for, though. Several men pounded around the corner of the house. One of them must have spotted the dark shape against the whitewashed wall, because he shouted, "There he is!"

"Get him!" ordered one of the other men, and orange flame spouted from gun muzzles as they opened fire.

Longarm threw himself headlong to the ground as bullets whistled over him. He landed on his belly and triggered a couple of fast shots, aiming low because he didn't want to kill any of Torrance's men if that could be avoided.

Another shot came from the window, kicking up dirt near Longarm's head. He rolled to his right. More bullets plowed the ground around him. Running footsteps pounded toward him from the other direction. Torrance's men had him surrounded now.

And that damned dog was struggling back to its feet already, a little shaky on its paws but still dangerous. The brute must have a skull like iron, thought Longarm as he lunged upright and sagged against the wall, hoping to hide for a moment in the shadows.

But there was no place to go, he saw. Torrance's men were all around him. Their guns had fallen silent as they realized they had him trapped. To reinforce that, Torrance called from the window, "Hold your fire, boys, unless he starts shootin' again." The rancher's voice was thick from the whiskey, but he didn't sound too drunk. He might be one of those little hombres who seemed to have a hollow leg when it came to booze.

"Toss that gun down, mister," ordered one of the men surrounding Longarm. "Do it now, or we'll blast the hell out of you."

Longarm had no doubt the man would be true to his word. With the bitter taste of failure in his mouth, Longarm leaned forward and dropped the Colt on the ground in front of him.

"Any other weapons?" asked the man who seemed to be the leader of Torrance's gunnies.

"That's it," Longarm said. When he was wearing his brown tweed suit, he usually carried a .41-caliber derringer in his vest pocket, attached by a chain to the Ingersoll watch that rode in his other vest pocket. But now he was dressed for the trail, in butternut shirt and denim trousers.

"Take him inside, to the boss's office."

A couple of the men holstered their guns and stepped forward to grab the intruder by the arms. A dozen or more of them still covered Longarm with their six-guns, so he didn't struggle as the two men hustled him toward the front of the house.

Followed closely by the members of Torrance's crew who had responded to the commotion, the men took Longarm inside, jerking him around and handling him roughly as they shoved him down a hallway. A moment later, he found himself in the room he had been looking into earlier. Bookshelves full of volumes bound in dark leather covered most of the wall space, but several brightly burning lamps kept the room from being too gloomy.

Cy Torrance stood beside the desk, his gun still in his hand. As Longarm had thought, he was small, an inch or two under medium height. Longarm hadn't been able to tell much about the way Torrance was built while the rancher was slumped in the chair, but now he could see that there was a considerable amount of wiry strength in Torrance's slender body.

And there was plenty of hatred in the man's dark, blazing eyes too.

"Who the hell are you?" demanded Torrance as he thrust the barrel of his revolver toward Longarm. "What are you doing here on my ranch?"

Longarm didn't see any point in obfuscation. He said, "My name's Custis Long. I'm a deputy United States marshal."

Several of the men who had crowded into the room behind him muttered curses at that revelation. Torrance frowned and barked, "A marshal! What's your business here?"

"I came to talk you out of making the worst mistake of your life, Torrance."

"You know who I am?"

Longarm nodded. "I know who you are, and I know what you've got planned for the town of Dry Creek."

Torrance's mouth twisted in a grimace under the gray mustache. "I should've known it!" he said. "I should've known those damned cowards would try to get out of what they got coming to them. I don't see how they sent for a lawman and got one here this fast, though."

"They didn't send for me," said Longarm. He wanted to keep Torrance talking, because the longer the conversation went on, the more chance he could get the man to see some reason. "I just happened to ride in there this afternoon and find out what's going on."

One of the men spoke up. "I told you somebody got past us, boss. Didn't have no idea it was a star packer."

Torrance looked at Longarm and snapped, "Who were the other two with you? More marshals?"

Again, nothing would be served by lying. "They were a couple of prisoners. They don't have anything to do with what happened in Dry Creek, Torrance."

"You mean my son being lynched? Thrown in jail for a crime he didn't commit, then dragged out and strung up from a tree?" Torrance snorted. "Seems to me that if you're really a lawman, mister, the ones you ought to be concerned with are the members of that lynch mob!"

Longarm nodded. "They'll answer for their crime, but right now I'm more worried about the innocent people in Dry Creek, the people who'll be killed if you make good on your threat to burn down the town and wipe out everybody in it."

"There aren't any innocent people in Dry Creek," snapped Torrance. "They all knew what was gonna happen to my boy. I've heard that they even had a damned town meeting about it!"

Longarm couldn't deny that, because Frank Webber had admitted as much to him. But he went at the problem from another direction, saying, "What about Lucy Kane?"

"Who?"

"The daughter of the woman who runs the café in town. She's nine or ten years old, Torrance. I don't reckon she had much to do with what happened to your son."

Torrance scowled. "That's a damned shame, but the gal's ma should have talked some sense into those bastards before they killed my boy."

"She tried. So did some of the other folks in town. Not everybody was in favor of what happened. The only way to make sure the ones who are really to blame are the only ones punished is to let the law handle it."

Torrance gave a snort of contempt. "The law! When I came out here and started the Rocking T, the closest law was in Wichita! You think I ran all the way back there cryin' for help every time I had a problem? The hell I did. I handled things myself. Still do."

"Times have changed—" Longarm began.

"But I haven't." Torrance made a curt gesture with his gun. "Lock him up, Jess."

The big man who had been giving orders earlier moved toward Longarm. That would be Jess Garth, Torrance's foreman, Longarm recalled from the story Webber had told him earlier.

Before Garth could lay hands on him, Longarm made a final try. "Look, you haven't harmed any innocents yet," he said to Torrance. "Eph Bridges was part of the group that hanged your son, so you might convince a judge that wasn't murder."

"Shut the hell up, mister," said Garth as he clasped his fingers around the butt of the gun on his hip. He drew it as if he intended to pistol-whip Longarm.

Torrance shot a hand out, motioning his foreman to a stop. "Hold it, Jess," he said. Then, frowning at Longarm, he asked, "What's this about Eph Bridges?"

"He's dead," said Longarm. "I reckon you know that, since it was probably some of your crew who strung him up."

"Strung him up?"

Longarm nodded. "That's right. From the branch of one of those cottonwood trees down by the creek."

"Just like Harry . . ." muttered Torrance. He seemed genuinely surprised by what Longarm had just told him.

Longarm frowned too. "Are you saying you didn't order Bridges's death?"

"I didn't know anything about it." Torrance looked at Garth. "How about you, Jess?"

"It's news to me, boss," rumbled Garth.

Longarm didn't know whether to believe them or not. Of course, it was possible that some of Torrance's men had killed Bridges anyway, without direct orders from the rancher. They were all familiar with Torrance's plans for Dry Creek, and they might have decided to take action on

94

their own, maybe in hopes of currying favor with their boss.

Or Torrance and Garth could be lying, Longarm told himself. He didn't know either of the men well enough to be a judge of their veracity.

Torrance flipped a hand, motioning the men out of the room. A couple of them grabbed Longarm and dragged him along. "Put him in the shed," Garth ordered. "And a couple of you stand guard over him. The boss don't want nobody interferin' with what he's got in mind for Dry Creek."

Unarmed and heavily outnumbered, Longarm had no choice but to cooperate, at least for the time being. He wasn't going to give up on his plan just yet, though. He still thought that if he could get out of here and take Torrance back to Dry Creek with him, he could turn this whole situation around.

And as he was shoved into a shed stacked high with bales of hay, he recalled what Torrance had said about not having anything to do with the murder of Eph Bridges. If that was true, it meant someone in Dry Creek had killed the liveryman. Who would have had a reason to do something like that?

The door of the shed was slammed shut. Total darkness enveloped Longarm. As far as he had been able to see, the door didn't have a bar or any other sort of lock to fasten it, just a simple latch to hold it closed. But Garth had posted guards just outside the door, in case Longarm tried to escape. Getting out wouldn't be easy.

Nothing much ever was, he reflected. Man was born to struggle, the Good Book said, and Longarm wasn't going to argue with Scripture. He sat down on one of the piles of hay bales and rested his hands on his knees.

An odd feeling had come over him. A nagging little voice in the back of his head told him that he had seen or heard something tonight that would cast everything else in a different light. He frowned in thought as he tried to figure out what it was. His hand stole up to his ear and tugged on the lobe in the involuntary habit that cropped up when his brain was working really hard. He ran his thumbnail along the line of his jaw, making a faint rasping sound as the nail dragged across beard stubble.

But no answers came, and with a sigh Longarm reached into his shirt pocket for a cheroot. He found one of the three-for-a-nickel smokes, put it in his mouth, and fished in his pocket for a lucifer.

He found one, but he didn't snap it into life with his thumbnail and set fire to the gasper. Instead, he sat there and smiled as an idea occurred to him. He might have come up with a way of getting out of here . . .

As long as it didn't kill him first.

Chapter 15

Longarm put the match back in his pocket for the moment, but left the cheroot in his mouth, unlit. He dragged the bales of hay away from the rear wall of the shed, hearing the skittering of rodents fleeing as he did so. Then he tore apart one of the bales, piling the loose hay along the base of the wall as he did so.

Dust from the hay tickled his nostrils as he worked. He hoped that he didn't stir up too much dust, because if he did, he ran the risk of causing an explosion when he lit the match. Sometimes on a really hot day, a barn full of hay would blow up on its own. All it took was the tiniest spark to ignite the dust and fumes in the air.

Well, if that happened, he told himself with a wry grin, it would probably blow the walls of the shed down. He'd get out of here one way or the other.

When he thought he had enough of the hay spread along the wall, he knelt beside it and took the match out again. Pausing before he lit it, he thought that it was possible Torrance would order his men to leave him in here. If that happened, the shed might burn down around his ears. Longarm thought that was unlikely, though. A cattleman's instinct would be to fight a fire and bring it under control, and besides, Torrance likely wouldn't want to lose the hay.

With a flick of Longarm's thumbnail, he lit the match and dropped it in the loose hay he had piled up along the base of the shed's rear wall.

The hay caught fire right away—without blowing up— and the flames spread quickly along the wall. The boards were dry enough that they began to burn fairly quickly. Smoke and heat rose from the blaze. Longarm backed away from it, coughing. "Hey!" he yelled through the door. "Hey, the place is on fire in here!"

He knew he'd had to take a chance on actually starting the fire. The guards wouldn't have believed him without the smoke to back him up.

Startled shouts came from outside. Longarm stepped to one side of the door as it crashed open. One of the guards ran into the shed. Longarm hoped the other one had gone to get help. He jumped the hombre who had just dashed inside.

A gun blasted from outside the door, and Longarm knew the second guard was still there. Longarm and the first guard went down as Longarm crashed into him from behind. The man tried to twist around and put up a fight, but he went limp as Longarm clubbed both hands together and smashed them into the back of his head.

The flames cast a hellish red glare over the inside of the shed, although the smoke made it a little difficult to see. The second guard tried to draw a bead on Longarm from the door and fired again. Longarm heard the wind-rip of the bullet's passage next to his ear as he rolled to one side, snagging the butt of the first guard's gun and jerking it from the holster as he went past the unconscious man. As he came over onto his back, Longarm lifted the weapon and pulled the trigger. The Colt bucked against the palm of his hand as a shot blasted. The second guard disappeared from the doorway, rocked backward by the bullet that punched into his shoulder.

Longarm scrambled to his feet. He bent down and grabbed the collar of the unconscious guard with his free hand. He wasn't going to leave the hombre here to burn up, no matter how big a varmint the fella might be.

Longarm stumbled out of the burning shed, dragging the guard with him. He let go of the man as soon as he was clear. The sharp sound of gunfire blended with the crackle of the flames. Longarm saw several men running toward him from the direction of the bunkhouse.

He ducked around the shed, putting it between him and the gunmen, and ran toward the two-story ranch house. While he wanted to get away from the Rocking T, he hadn't completely given up on his idea of taking Torrance back to Dry Creek with him.

There was a side porch on the part of the house facing toward him. He ignored the steps and leaped onto the porch in a single bound. His shoulder crashed against the door leading into the house, knocking it open. He ran in and found himself in a corridor that led toward the center of the house, past a dining room. A small lamp burned up ahead, showing him the base of the stairs from the second floor. When Longarm got there, instead of ascending the stairs, he turned toward another hallway that he recognized from earlier in the night. Torrance's office was down there.

Torrance might not be brooding and drinking in the office anymore, but that was the first place Longarm figured to look. As he started in that direction, though, Jess Garth appeared at the top of the stairs. Torrance's foreman roared a curse and started throwing lead with the heavy six-gun in his hand.

Longarm went to the side in a rolling dive, came up firing through the railing of the staircase. Garth yelled in pain as one of the lawman's slugs burned across his left thigh. He clapped a hand to the wound, but his leg was already giving way beneath him. Garth fell with a heavy thud.

Even down, he was still dangerous. His gun roared

again as Longarm scrambled up. The slug plowed into the floor, but well behind Longarm, who had seen the door of the office start to swing open. He charged toward it and ran into Torrance just as the rancher stepped out into the hall.

Longarm was quite a bit bigger and heavier than Torrance, and he had some momentum built up. Torrance went over backward as Longarm crashed into him, and would have fallen to be trampled under the lawman's boots if Longarm hadn't grabbed him around the waist with his left arm. Longarm went straight across the room to the window, taking Torrance with him. Glass shattered and wood splintered as they smashed through it, toppling to the ground outside the house.

Torrance seemed to be stunned into insensibility by the impact, and Longarm was a mite shaken up himself. But he knew he couldn't afford to waste time gathering his wits. He shoved himself to his feet, jammed the revolver he had taken from the guard into his holster, and picked up Torrance as if the rancher had been little more than a child. With barely a grunt of effort, Longarm slung Torrance over his shoulder and took off in a run toward the place where he had left his horse. Though it seemed like hours since he had told the blaze-faced gelding to stay put, actually it had been only about half an hour. The horse might still be there.

Longarm was betting his life that it would be.

A few more shots blasted behind him, but then over the pounding of his feet on the earth and the hammering of his pulse inside his head, he heard Jess Garth bellowing, "Hold your fire! Hold your fire, damn it! The bastard's got the boss with him!"

A savage grin stretched across Longarm's face. He had hoped that by grabbing Torrance he would keep the Rocking T men from gunning him down.

"Saddle some horses!" shouted Garth. "Blast it, *move*!"

It was hard to believe that only about twenty-four hours

had passed since Longarm had made his stealthy approach toward the soddy where he had tracked Tom Rankin. Those hours had been packed with action and emotion, and they were beginning to take a toll even on Longarm's iron constitution.

But he still had some reserves of strength left, and he drew on them now, calling on those inner resources to give him the speed he needed. The low-heeled boots he wore were better suited to running than the high-heeled boots most cowboys wore, but even so they weren't made for such activities. His feet already hurt, and the muscles of his legs felt like lead. Plus he had the weight of Cy Torrance on his shoulder slowing him down. But he summoned up the strength to keep moving, and after a few moments he spotted a dark shape in the moonlight that he recognized as the gelding. The horse tried to shy away as Longarm ran toward him, but the trailing reins made him stop when Longarm stepped on them.

Longarm stumbled to a halt and reached for the reins, saying in a low, reassuring voice, "Take it easy, old son, just take it easy there." He caught the reins and pulled them tight. Then he lifted Torrance and slung the rancher across the horse's back, just in front of the McClellan saddle. Longarm got his left foot in the stirrup and swung up onto the gelding.

The horse wasn't too fond of the idea of carrying double like that, especially when one of the riders was limp and unconscious, but Longarm's firm hand on the reins kept him under control. Longarm turned the horse toward Dry Creek. His heels urged the gelding into a run.

He had no doubt that Torrance's men would come after them, and their mounts might be fresher. But Longarm still had Torrance with him, so the Rocking T men couldn't start firing as soon as they came in sight of him. They would still have to hold their fire or risk hitting their boss, and Longarm didn't think they'd want to do that.

All he had to do was reach Dry Creek with Torrance before the pursuers could get close enough to dab a loop on him or risk shooting the horse out from under him. Then he could start trying to figure out a way to bring this mess to a conclusion without a lot more killing.

Torrance stirred suddenly, writhing around and sputtering. Longarm drew the Colt and put the muzzle against the back of his neck, saying, "Settle down, mister. I don't want to shoot you, but I'll sure clout you with the butt of this sixshooter if I have to."

Torrance grew still. After a few moments, he called over the drumming of the gelding's hoofbeats, "Let me up, damn you! I'm getting sick!"

After all the trouble Torrance had caused, Longarm didn't much care whether he got sick or not, but on the other hand, he didn't want Torrance puking all over his foot either. He hauled back on the reins, bringing the gelding to a halt. Then he grabbed hold of Torrance's shirt collar and threw him onto the ground.

Torrance landed hard, knocking the breath out of him. As the rancher gasped for air, Longarm said, "You're smart enough to know I need to keep you alive, Torrance. But if you give me any trouble, I'll put a bullet through your knee. You'll never walk right again, and maybe never ride again either."

"Damn you, Long," said Torrance as he climbed shakily to his feet. "You can't get away with this. I'm the richest man in these parts—"

"That don't excuse killing a man and threatening to burn a town to the ground and murder everybody in it."

"I tell you, I didn't have anything to do with Eph Bridges getting strung up! And as for the other . . . well, I haven't done it yet, have I?"

"You told the folks in Dry Creek that you were going to. You've got those poor folks living in terror."

"They deserve to be scared, after what they did to my boy."

Longarm didn't waste any more time arguing. He gestured with the gun and said, "Give me your hand. You can ride in front of me. But don't try anything, or *you're* the one who'll be sorry."

Torrance hesitated, then reached up and took Longarm's outstretched left hand. Awkwardly, he climbed onto the gelding's back. "You're going to regret this," he said.

"I already do," said Longarm. "I wish I'd never heard of you or your son or Dry Creek. But it's too late for that now, ain't it?"

He heeled the gelding into motion again and urged it into a gallop, heading due south toward the settlement where the citizens waited anxiously for the terrible vengeance promised by the man who rode with him.

Chapter 16

Torrance didn't try anything. Longarm was ready to wallop him again and knock him out if he did. But after several minutes of silence, Torrance said, "So Eph Bridges is dead, huh?"

"That's right."

"Strung up from a cottonwood tree?"

"Yep."

Torrance was quiet again for a moment; then he said, "I liked old Eph, but he had it comin'. Him and Everett and Yates and all the others. And Frank Webber, for letting them do what they did."

"But you didn't have anything to do with Bridges's death," said Longarm, his tone openly skeptical.

Torrance twisted his neck to look back over his shoulder. "I damn sure didn't," he declared. "I'm not saying Eph and the others didn't deserve something like that, but it's not the way I do things. When I've got a score to settle, I do it out in the open, where everybody can see. That's the way I've always been, and I'm too old to change now."

"If you didn't order Bridges's hanging, then some of your crew did it on their own."

Torrance shook his head. "They wouldn't do that. I pay my men well enough so's they'd charge hell with a bucket of water if I told 'em to, but they don't do anything unless me or Jess tell them to."

"What if Garth ordered the hanging?"

"He was out at the ranch headquarters with me all evening, and all day before that." Torrance snorted. "Trying to talk me out of razing the town."

Longarm found that interesting. "So Garth's not going along with your plan?"

"Oh, he'll go along with whatever I say. Jess rides for the brand. But that doesn't mean he has to like everything that I decide."

Longarm nodded as he filed away that bit of information, in case later on he needed to try to drive a wedge between Torrance and Garth.

After a moment, Torrance went on. "The last time Jess spoke up against me was five years ago. I'd been having some trouble with a fella who had a little spread adjoining some of my range. He'd been rustling my stock for a long time. I tried to get him to sell out to me, made him a fair offer, a lot better offer than he deserved, but he wouldn't do it. Said he could never leave that land."

Longarm was curious in spite of himself. "Why not?"

Torrance shrugged and said, "His wife had died. She was buried there."

"But you didn't care about that," said Longarm.

"He stole from me!" Torrance responded in indignation. "Besides, he had a damn fine spring on his place."

"And you wanted it."

"Cows need water," Torrance bit off.

"I suppose you got your hands on the fella's spread sooner or later."

"Damn right. One night, me and some of the boys rode over there and burned down his cabin. He saw then that he'd do well to take my offer. He signed a bill of sale."

"Garth didn't think you ought to burn down a man's home?"

"Jess was fine with that," said Torrance. "He didn't like it when I had the stubborn bastard horse-whipped."

Longarm stiffened. "You had the man whipped *after* he'd signed his ranch over to you?"

"He had it coming," snapped Torrance, using what seemed to be his favorite phrase for justifying anything he wanted to do. "The man defied me, stole from me. I couldn't let him get away with that. If I had, every nester and greasy-sack outfit in this whole end of the state would be tryin' to move in on me."

Longarm didn't say anything. Torrance's arrogance was sickening.

When he thought it over, though, and remembered other things he had been told tonight, he asked, "That was Eph Bridges you were talking about, wasn't it?"

"What? Bridges? Hell, no. Bridges had a little spread that I bought too, but he didn't have to be burned out and whipped. That was somebody else entirely."

"No wonder folks around here hate you."

"I don't give a damn whether or not they hate me, as long as they're afraid of me."

"Well, you succeeded there," said Longarm. He had spotted the lights of Dry Creek up ahead. "Maybe I ought to just turn you over to them and let them do whatever they want with you."

Torrance turned to look at him again, and this time there was a nervous edge in the rancher's voice as he said, "You can't do that. You're a marshal. You're sworn to uphold the law."

"That don't mean I can't look the other way every now and then."

Torrance muttered a curse and fell silent. Longarm wouldn't actually turn him over to the citizens of Dry Creek, but Torrance didn't have to know that.

Longarm had kept the gelding moving at a fast pace, and he had watched their back trail for signs of pursuit during the ride to town. The moonlight was bright enough now that he could see a plume of dust rising into the air about half a mile behind them. That would be Jess Garth and the rest of the Rocking T crew, he thought. But Dry Creek was close enough now so that Longarm was confident he and Torrance would reach the settlement before Torrance's men caught up to them.

The pursuit wasn't the only danger abroad in the night, though. Torrance also had men riding patrols around the town to keep anyone from leaving—although they hadn't been very successful at that earlier in the evening when Longarm left Dry Creek. He fully expected to run into one of those patrols on the way back into town, and sure enough, a few minutes later he heard the drumming of hoofbeats nearby.

He nudged Torrance and said, "Better sing out and let your boys know that it's you. If they start burning powder, they're just as liable to shoot you as me."

"Go to hell," snapped Torrance. "I'll take my chances."

"Suit yourself," said Longarm. He dug his heels into the gelding's flanks, calling on the gallant animal to deliver one last burst of speed.

The gelding lunged forward, stretching out into a hard gallop. Nearby, a man yelled, "Hey! Hold it! Stop, damn it, or we'll shoot!"

Longarm didn't slow the horse. He let the gelding have its head and leaned forward, forcing Torrance to lean over the horse's neck too. Flame geysered from the muzzles of pistols to their right.

Longarm veered the gelding to the left, away from the gunfire, but realized a second later that was exactly what Torrance's men wanted him to do. Three riders loomed up in that direction, moving fast to intercept him. They blocked his path with their horses, and Longarm had no choice but to pull back hard on the reins and haul the gelding around in a skidding, leaning turn.

As he was doing that, Torrance suddenly drove an elbow back into Longarm's belly. He yelled, "Hold your fire! It's me, Torrance!" and tried to leap off the horse.

Longarm recovered from the blow just in time to loop his right arm around Torrance's neck and jerk him back. He had his gun in that hand and the reins in the left. As Torrance writhed and struggled, trying to get free, Longarm let go of him for a second, just long enough to slap the barrel of his gun against Torrance's skull above the right ear. Torrance slumped forward, stunned, and would have slipped off the gelding's back if Longarm hadn't grabbed him again.

Torrance's outcry had warned his men of his presence, and they stopped shooting for fear of hitting him. That was one advantage Longarm had. But they were still all around him, closing in from two directions now.

He whirled the gelding again and started back in the direction he had come from. Garth and the rest of the Rocking T crew were galloping in from that quarter, so Longarm knew he couldn't escape that way. But he was counting on their presence to confuse the issue a little, just enough to give him a chance of slipping out of this trap. He jerked the gelding sharply to the left, cutting across the face of the pursuit.

Now there were hoofbeats everywhere as the three groups of riders converged. Men shouted questions, and even though a couple of different voices, including Jess Garth's, bellowed for them to hold their fire, a couple of nervous hombres jerked their triggers anyway. The shots led to more shouting.

And all the while, Longarm had pulled the gelding back to a walk, so he wasn't making nearly as much noise as everybody else out here as he headed toward the line of trees that marked the course of the stream known as Dry Creek.

Seconds dragged out and seemed like minutes as they passed. Torrance was still unconscious, and Longarm hoped that clouting the man twice like that hadn't done any permanent damage to his brain. If that proved to be the case, though, then Torrance had brought that fate on himself. Longarm was trying to save the lives of a whole town full of people, so Torrance had to take his chances.

The trees drew closer and closer, and Torrance's men were still milling around. Longarm held his breath as the gelding neared the creek.

Then someone yelled from behind, "There they go!" Instantly, with a rumble of hoofbeats like the sound of distant drums, the gunmen gave chase.

Longarm kicked the gelding into a run again. The trees were only about twenty yards away, with the stream just beyond them. Longarm knew the banks were fairly steep in places, so he would just have to hope that the horse could make it down the near one and up the far one before the pursuers caught up to them.

They flashed through the line of cottonwoods, and Longarm saw the shallow creek in front of them. The bank right here was only about four feet high. The blaze-faced gelding didn't even slow down. He leaped from the bank, landed in the middle of the stream with a huge splash, and leaped again, clearing the south bank with ease. Another dash through the trees, and they were on the edge of the settlement.

"Hold your fire!" shouted Longarm, knowing there were guards posted over here. "It's Marshal Long! Hold your fire!"

No one shot at him as he reached the rear of the buildings on the north side of Main Street. He slowed the horse to a walk as he went down an alley. Torrance was beginning to stir. Longarm prodded him in the back with the Colt and warned, "Don't try to cause a ruckus again, Torrance. I'd hate to have to slug you a third time."

"Go to . . . hell," Torrance muttered. He shook his head slowly, probably trying to dislodge some of the cobwebs from his brain. "Lord, my head hurts."

"You should've thought about that before you threatened to wipe out a whole town," said Longarm.

When he rode out onto the street, he found several men waiting for him, carrying rifles. He recognized Everett, the owner of the Plaza Hotel, among them.

"Marshal Long, is that really you?" Everett asked.

"It's me," replied Longarm, "and I've got Torrance with me."

That brought startled exclamations from the men. "What are you going to do with him?" asked one of them.

"Keep trying to talk some sense into his head, I reckon. But the main thing is, his men won't be very likely to attack the town while they know we've got him."

Mutters of agreement came from the townsmen. Longarm had been listening for shots from the direction of the creek, but so far, none had sounded. He suspected that Jess Garth realized he'd made it into the settlement with Torrance as his prisoner. Garth was probably sitting out there on the prairie with the rest of the Rocking T crew, trying to figure out what the hell he was supposed to do next.

Longarm turned the gelding toward the jail. The men walked alongside him as he rode in that direction, and Everett said, "Marshal Webber didn't think you were coming back. He was afraid you'd gotten killed out there at the Rocking T. So he came up with another idea."

"What's that?" asked Longarm.

"He thought we ought to all ride out there together and take the fight to Torrance. Try to wipe him out before he could attack the town."

Longarm frowned. That was a damned foolish idea, and likely all it would accomplish would be to get these folks killed even sooner. But he supposed Webber was just about at the end of his rope and was ready to try anything, no matter how reckless and foolhardy it might be.

Such a desperate move wouldn't be necessary now that Longarm had brought Torrance back to town with him. Dry Creek was still under siege, but Longarm was counting on the fact that the gunmen wouldn't be likely to attack as long as their boss was held hostage. The longer he could postpone the showdown, the greater the chance that he could head it off entirely.

He reined to a stop in front of the jail and swung down first, then stepped back and told Torrance to dismount. The townsmen gathered around, muttering angrily, and Longarm sensed that they would like nothing better than to grab Torrance and settle the score for what he had done. As far as these men knew, the rancher was responsible for the death of Eph Bridges, and despite Torrance's denial, Longarm wasn't completely convinced they weren't right.

That could all be hashed out later. For now, Longarm wanted to get Torrance in a safe place, and he figured the marshal's office would be best. "Let's go," he said as he grasped Torrance's shoulder and steered him toward the door of the building. He moved up close behind Torrance to prevent anyone else from grabbing him.

Longarm was a little surprised that Marshal Webber hadn't come out of the office to see what all the commotion was about. The lamp was burning inside, so he figured Webber was there.

As Longarm reached past Torrance to open the door, he saw why Webber hadn't put in an appearance yet. The marshal was stretched out facedown on the floor, with a thin trickle of blood running from a cut on his forehead where someone had hit him. Alarmed, Longarm shoved Torrance into the room and hurried to Webber's side as the rest of the men crowded into the office behind them. "What the hell!" one of them said.

Longarm dropped to a knee and took hold of Webber's

shoulder, rolling the local lawman onto his back. Webber let out a groan and his eyelids fluttered as consciousness began to return to him. Longarm figured that he would be all right, that he had just been knocked out.

And Longarm had no doubt who had done it, because as he glanced toward the single cell, he saw that the barred door stood open and the cell was empty.

Tom Rankin was gone.

Chapter 17

Longarm helped Webber sit up. The marshal shook his head groggily, blinked his eyes at Longarm, and rasped, "What the hell happened?"

"I was about to ask you the same question, old son."

Webber reached up, touched the bloody place on his head, and winced. "That son of a bitch," he said.

"Rankin?"

"Yeah. I came in and the bastard had hanged himself from the bars in the door."

Another hanged man, Longarm thought bitterly. Was there no end to them?

"How in blazes did he manage to do that?"

"Tore strips off the blanket on the cot and tied them together to make a rope, looked like. Anyway, I seen he was still alive, but he was chokin' and his tongue was stickin' out and his face was turnin' blue. I thought I might be able to save him, so I unlocked the cell as fast as I could and rushed in there to grab him and lift him up."

"And when you did that, he grabbed your gun and walloped you, because he wasn't actually choking after all." It wasn't really a guess, as Longarm's grim, flat tone indicated.

115

Webber nodded, looking and sounding disgusted with himself as he said, "Yeah. I should've known it was a trick. I ain't been a lawman all my life, but I've carried a badge long enough not to be fooled like that."

Longarm didn't want to make excuses for Webber, because he knew the marshal was right, but he said, "You've been under a hell of a strain lately, and Lord knows when you slept the last time. We all make mistakes."

"I reckon. I'd say I'm damned lucky Rankin didn't kill me. He was probably in too much of a hurry for that, just wanted to get outta here as fast as he could." Webber looked around the room and seemed to notice Longarm's prisoner for the first time. "Torrance! By God, you brought him back, Marshal!"

"Yeah," said Longarm as he helped Webber to his feet, "and since that cell is empty, I think it'd be a good idea to lock him up."

"I'd be plumb happy to," said Webber with a note of satisfaction in his voice. "Torrance has been runnin' roughshod over folks around here for a long time. He should've been behind bars a long time ago for some of the things he's done."

Thinking about the story Torrance had told him about burning out and whipping a rival rancher, Longarm nodded. He said, "The main thing is, as long as we've got him here in town, his gunmen aren't very likely to attack."

Torrance sneered. "That's where you're wrong, mister. Jess Garth knows what I had in mind for this town. As soon as he thinks it over, he'll know what I'd want him to do. The score will be settled with Dry Creek, no matter what happens to me."

Webber grabbed his arm and shoved him toward the cell. "Get in there and shut up. Your day's over, Torrance."

The rancher glared at him through slitted eyes. "You'll be sorry you crossed me again, Webber. Remember what happened last time?"

Webber's face flushed a deep red with anger. He shoved Torrance again, this time all the way into the cell. The door clanged shut behind the rancher.

Webber turned back to Longarm and said, "You reckon Rankin tried to get out of town? If he did, he's liable to run into Torrance's men."

"I haven't heard any shooting out there, except when they were trying to stop me from getting into town with Torrance. Rankin may still be around somewhere, lying low." An idea occurred to Longarm. "In fact, I know where he might be. If you can keep an eye on Torrance, I'll go have a look."

"I can come with you," offered Webber.

Longarm shook his head. "I'd rather you stay here." He shot a meaningful look in the direction of Everett and the other townsmen, who were still glaring angrily at Torrance and muttering among themselves.

A look of understanding appeared on Webber's face. He said, "Yeah, you don't have to worry about anything, Long. I'll guard the jail."

Longarm nodded. After what had happened to Harry Torrance, he didn't think that Webber would allow another lynching to take place.

Just to increase the odds against it, he ushered the townies out and told them to go back to standing guard, in case Torrance's men did try to pull something. They left, reluctantly, and Longarm headed toward the Plaza Hotel.

Rankin had known Mollie Bramlett for only a day, and he hadn't even gone to bed with her. Sure, he had promised to take her to San Francisco with him, but Longarm had never thought that Rankin would keep that promise. Would the outlaw risk his neck to free her? It seemed unlikely, but there was just enough of a chance he would that Longarm believed it was worth checking out.

The hotel lobby was deserted as Longarm entered it. He drew the Colt as he started up the stairs. The gun was the

117

same model as the one he normally carried, so he hadn't had to get used to it and the cartridges in his shell belt fit it just fine.

He flexed the fingers of his left hand. That hand was starting to get sore from the dog bite, but for now he had to ignore it. He wished he'd had a chance to pour some whiskey over the wounds that the cur's teeth had left. And he hoped the son of a bitch was just mean and didn't have hydrophobia. That was the last thing he needed right about now.

As he reached the second-floor landing, he slipped his left hand in his pocket and found the key to Room Seven, which Everett had given him earlier in the evening. He tapped on the door with the barrel of his gun and called, "Miz Bramlett? You in there?"

"What do you want, Marshal?" she replied in a dull, lifeless voice.

"Have you seen Tom Rankin?"

"Not since you locked him up. Why would I have seen Rankin? Did he escape?"

Longarm didn't answer that question. Instead, he said, "Step away from the door, ma'am. I'm coming in to have a look around."

He put the key in the lock and turned it, and the rattling sound that it made almost covered up the faint squeak of a floorboard somewhere behind him. Despite that, Longarm's keen ears heard the sound anyway, and instinct sent warning bells clanging through his brain. He twisted away from the door.

The corridor behind him was still empty, but even as his senses registered that, a dull boom shook the hallway and a huge hole appeared in the door of the room opposite. Someone in that room had just fired a shotgun through the door at close range, and the double load of buckshot whistled across the hall and tore a similar hole in the door of Room Seven. If Longarm had still been standing there unlocking it, the hole would be through him too.

118

Instead, only a couple of pellets had struck him as he flung himself out of the line of fire, and as he hit the carpet runner in the center of the hallway, he looked through the gaping hole in the opposite door and saw Tom Rankin standing there. When Rankin saw that Longarm had escaped the double-barreled blast, the outlaw dropped the empty shotgun and clawed at the holstered revolver on his hip.

Longarm fired before Rankin cleared leather, triggering twice. Both bullets caught the outlaw in the chest and drove him backward. Rankin stumbled and went down.

Longarm surged up from the floor, grabbed the knob of the buckshot-shattered door, and threw it open. He kept the Colt trained on Rankin as he hurried over to the man and kicked aside the revolver that Rankin had dropped without ever firing it. Rankin's boot heels drummed on the floorboards and his back arched up from the rug as his dying spasms shook him. His eyes were open, and he lived long enough to send a hate-filled glare at Longarm before his final breath rattled in his throat and he slumped back to the floor. The sharp stink of his voiding bowels filled the room.

Longarm wheeled around, not wasting any more time on Rankin. He hurried across the corridor. The double charge of buckshot had been spreading as it struck the door of Room Seven, and it had punched through the thin panel in so many places that the door literally fell apart as Longarm opened it. He stepped into the room, his face grim.

He saw what he expected to see. Mollie Bramlett had been standing in front of the window when Rankin fired. The glass was shattered now, and what was left of the frame was splashed with crimson. Mollie lay on the floor. Her dress had half a dozen or more spreading bloodstains on it where the pellets had ripped through her. A bubbling cough shook her as Longarm hurried across the room to kneel beside her.

He slipped a hand under her head and lifted it. Blood

ran from her mouth. She struggled to open her eyes, and when she did, she looked up at Longarm and tried to form words.

"Rest easy," he told her. "You're not hurt bad."

It was a lie, of course. She had only minutes, perhaps seconds, of life remaining to her. But he hoped she was too far gone to realize that.

In a thick, strained voice, she managed to say, "Should . . . should've . . ."

Longarm leaned closer. "Should've what, ma'am?"

She coughed again, and more blood welled from her mouth. She gurgled, "Should've never shot my husband."

That effort took the last of her strength. Her eyes rolled up in their sockets and her head fell to the side as the muscles in her neck went limp. Longarm lowered her as gently as he could, even though she could no longer feel it.

Rankin had known that he would come here to check on Mollie, he thought. The outlaw had waited across the hall for him with a shotgun and a revolver he had taken from the marshal's office after knocking Webber out.

If Rankin had tried to get out of Dry Creek, he might have been successful. Instead, he had allowed his desire for vengeance on Longarm to make him linger and set that trap, and he had paid for the decision with his life. But Mollie Bramlett had paid the ultimate price too.

Or maybe in her case, the toll had finally come due, mused Longarm. She had started down this path the night before, when she'd decided to put a bullet in her husband's back. It had just taken a little more than twenty-four hours for fate to catch up with her.

He couldn't bring himself to feel particularly satisfied about any of it, though. Some folks might think that justice had been done. To him, it seemed more like a damned shame all the way around.

He sighed and stood up, and as he did so Marshal Webber appeared in the shattered doorway, holding a rifle.

"Heard the shots," explained the star packer. He grimaced as he looked at Mollie's bloody form. "What happened?"

Longarm nodded toward the room across the hall and said, "Rankin's in there. He was waiting for me to come here and check on Mrs. Bramlett. When I did, he tried to blow me in two with a Greener."

Webber looked back and forth between the two buckshot-riddled doors and said, "Looks like he came damned close to succeedin' too."

"Yeah. I was lucky this time. A hell of a lot luckier than Mrs. Bramlett." Longarm thumbed fresh shells into the Colt. "Better get the local undertaker up here. He'll have plenty of work to keep him busy the rest of the night, I reckon."

"What about Torrance?"

"I'll go back to the jail and keep an eye on him." A worried frown appeared on Longarm's rugged face. "He shouldn't have been left alone for this long."

"Well, excuse me all to hell for thinkin' you might've got yourself blowed up," snapped Webber. "I heard what sounded like a war breakin' out and thought I'd better take a look."

"Sorry, Marshal," muttered Longarm. "Go on and fetch the undertaker."

Webber nodded curtly and headed down the stairs. Longarm took one last look at Rankin and Mollie and then followed him.

There was nothing more he could do here, and the threat of Torrance's vengeance still hung over Dry Creek.

Chapter 18

To Longarm's relief, Torrance was still in the cell inside the marshal's office, and it didn't appear that anyone had bothered him. The citizens probably hadn't realized that Webber had left him alone. Either that, or they were still reluctant to cross Longarm.

Torrance glared through the bars at him as he came in. "Sounded like all hell broke loose," the rancher said. "For a second there, I thought Jess and the boys were coming in."

"No such luck for you," said Longarm. "How do they know we won't just go ahead and kill you if they attack?"

"They don't. But Jess knows one thing. I'd rather be dead than let this town get away with what it did to my son."

Longarm shook his head. He supposed he could comprehend what Torrance was feeling, but he would never fully understand it. No matter what happened to the citizens of Dry Creek, it wouldn't bring Harry Torrance back to life.

Webber returned to the marshal's office a short time later, with the rifle tucked under his arm. "The undertaker and his helpers have gone up to the hotel to fetch the bodies," he said. "I can take over again now, if you want to get some rest, Marshal."

Longarm had gone past the point of being tired hours earlier. He was well on his way to exhaustion now. He nodded and stretched to ease weary muscles.

"I'll take you up on that. Maybe Everett's got another empty room in the hotel he'll let me have for the night." Longarm pulled the Ingersoll from the watch pocket in his trousers and flipped it open. He was a mite surprised to see that it was only one o'clock in the morning. As busy as the night had been, and as tired as he was, it seemed more like the hour ought to be approaching dawn.

That thought reminded him of Jess Garth and the Rocking T gunmen who were lurking somewhere outside the settlement. He motioned for Webber to follow him onto the porch, and when they were out of earshot of Torrance, he said, "Don't let me sleep more than three hours or so. I want to be up before dawn, because if Garth decides to attack, that's likely when it'll be."

"You think that's likely to happen as long as we've got Torrance as our prisoner?"

"You wouldn't think so, but like Torrance told me, Garth knows how badly Torrance wants to take his revenge on this town. I wouldn't bet my life that he and the rest of those gun wolves *won't* come in."

Webber nodded. "Bettin' our lives is exactly what we've been doin' all along, seems to me like."

He had a point there, thought Longarm. With a nod, he started off toward the hotel.

His weariness almost caught up with him before he got there. When he came into the lobby, he was on the verge of nodding off while still on his feet. Everett was there, and the proprietor gave him the key to Room Fourteen.

"It's right on the front, Marshal," Everett explained. "If there's any trouble, you ought to hear it."

"I don't know," said Longarm. "As tired as I am, once I

go to sleep I ain't sure even a cyclone would wake me up."

He managed to stay awake until he reached the room on the second floor, down the hall beyond the rooms where Tom Rankin and Mollie Bramlett had died. Longarm didn't glance into either of those rooms as he trudged past them. He didn't need any reminders of what had happened here.

When he reached Room Fourteen, he went inside and locked the door behind him, then without bothering to light the lamp he fell fully clothed onto the bed. He was asleep mere moments after his head hit the pillow.

Longarm had told Webber to wake him in about three hours, but it seemed more like three minutes when his eyes snapped open and his senses sprang to full alert. His hand shot out and closed around the butt of the Colt as he rolled over. The gun came up and his finger tightened on the trigger as the barrel lined up with the dark shape that stood just inside the door of the room.

"Custis!" Deborah Kane cried out in alarm.

Longarm held off firing, but just barely. His pulse hammered in his head as he brought his instincts under control. "Good Lord, gal!" he burst out. "I damn near shot you!"

Deborah came closer to the bed. "I'm sorry. I didn't mean to cause a problem, Custis. I just . . . had to see you again."

Longarm lowered the Colt and then slid the iron back into leather. "What time is it?"

"A little after three thirty."

Longarm nodded. He would have been getting up in another half hour or so anyway, so he hadn't lost all that much sleep.

But that didn't explain what Deborah was doing here, and Longarm wondered as well where her little girl was.

"She's asleep on the sofa in the lobby downstairs," replied Deborah when Longarm asked her about Lucy. "Mr. Everett is watching her."

"You gathered her up and brought her out in the middle of the night?"

Deborah sat down on the edge of the bed and knotted her hands together. "I know, I'm a terrible mother. We're all facing such danger that we may not survive another day, and yet, like you said, I bundled Lucy up and came out in the night because . . . because of what I felt for a man . . ."

Longarm frowned. "You're saying . . ."

"I'm saying I couldn't face the prospect of dying without having you make love to me one more time, Custis." She gave a hollow laugh. "You've awakened something inside me that's been asleep for a long time, ever since my husband died, in fact. Maybe even before that. I felt things with you that I . . . I never experienced before. And I need to feel them again, one last time."

Longarm was still worn out. A few hours of sleep hadn't been enough to restore all his strength, and he was still facing all kinds of problems, including possible mortal danger.

And yet he knew what Deborah meant. The bond between a man and a woman was sometimes so strong that it overpowered everything else, up to and including good sense.

"Who knows you're here besides Everett?" he asked.

"Well, Marshal Webber is the only one, I suppose. I went to the marshal's office to look for you first, and he said you'd come down here to get some rest before dawn, in case Torrance's men attack then."

"You know that word of this is going to get around, don't you? It ain't gonna help your reputation, you being a widow lady and all."

Deborah smiled. Longarm could see her face in the light that filtered in through the thin curtains.

"Maybe we'll be lucky," she said as she moved closer to him. "Maybe we'll all be wiped out, and I won't have to worry about my reputation."

Longarm chuckled at the dark humor and put his arms around her. He was powerfully drawn to her too, and if he was going to die, there were worse ways to spend some of his final moments on earth.

He kissed her, and her lips parted to welcome his tongue. After a moment, she pulled back a little and whispered, "I want to do everything, Custis. Anything you can think of, I want to experience it."

"That's a mighty tall order," he said, "considering it's only about an hour until dawn."

"Well, then, let's get in as much as possible."

Longarm was up to that challenge. They didn't waste any more time on words, but instead spent the next few minutes stripping off each other's clothes. When they were both naked, he laid her back on the bed, spread her legs, and kissed and licked his way up her inner thighs from her knees to the highly sensitive center of her femininity. He opened the folds of her sex with his thumbs and ran his tongue along them, from the bottom to the top, lingering to suck the insistent little bud of flesh between his lips. As she moaned and pushed her groin against his face, he slipped a hand underneath her and found the tight, puckered opening even farther down. Enough of his spit and her juices ran down there so that he was able to slide his middle finger into her and slowly rotate it, stretching the constricted passage. Deborah groaned in delight.

Longarm continued pleasuring her with his fingers, lips, and tongue for long, delicious minutes, until spasms of ecstasy began to roll through her. When that tidal wave of culmination finally subsided, she drew in deep, shuddering breaths and said, "Now . . . now it's . . . your turn, Custis."

Longarm wasn't going to argue. He let her roll him over onto his back. His erect member stood up tall and straight and proud. Deborah turned so that she could grasp it with both hands. She held it with one and began to pump up and down with the other, while at the same time she pressed her lips to the tip. After a moment, she flicked her tongue against the slitlike opening, then opened her mouth and took the entire crown into it. The shaft was so thick that it filled her mouth, and she could swallow only a few inches of it without choking.

But she made the most of those few inches, swirling her tongue around the head and sucking gently on it. As her urgency grew, she became not quite so gentle, but Longarm didn't complain. She kept milking his cock with one hand while the other stole down and cupped the heavy balls at the base, rolling them back and forth in her palm.

Longarm closed his eyes and lay back to enjoy what she was doing to him. She was a little awkward at times, as if she didn't have much practice at this, but that was just endearingly innocent. To Longarm's way of thinking, there was nothing quite as good as having a tender, sweet-faced woman sucking his cock.

Unless it was putting his rock-hard shaft inside that woman, which was exactly what he was ready to do after a while. Deborah was ready to have it inside her too, as she demonstrated by lifting her head and swinging a leg over his hips. As she straddled him, she reached down to grip his pole and guide it to her well-soaked opening. With a downward thrust of her hips, she impaled herself on him.

Longarm bucked up into her as she braced herself with her hands on his chest and began pumping her hips. She rode him hard, like she was galloping for the finish line in a high-stakes race. The fleeting thought that the stakes *were* pretty high crossed Longarm's mind. This might be the last time for both of them.

Because of that, he wanted to make it last, but the tide of passion that washed through him was just too strong. He grabbed hold of her breasts as they bobbed above him, filling his hands with the soft woman flesh. He thumbed her hard nipples. She panted and cried out, and suddenly she began to jerk and shudder. Longarm's climax had exploded on him without warning too, and his juices erupted hotly inside her. Spasm after throbbing spasm emptied him.

Deborah said, "Ohhhhh . . ." and slumped forward onto his chest. He put his arms around her and held her as a few final shudders went through both of them. Longarm's chest rose and fell heavily as his heart pounded. He stroked Deborah's quivering flanks.

When she recovered enough to speak again, she said, "I . . . I can die a happy woman now . . ."

But despite her words, she began to cry.

Longarm's embrace tightened around her. "It'll be all right," he told her. "It'll be all right."

He had no idea how he was going to keep that promise, but he was going to do everything in his power to make it come true.

They might have stayed there like that for longer, but the sound of loud voices came to his ears, drifting in through the small gap where the window was raised a couple of inches. Deborah heard the commotion too, and lifted her head.

"What's that?"

Longarm said, "I don't know, but I reckon I ought to find out." He rolled to the side, taking her with him, and then pushed himself up and off her, feeling a twinge of regret as his softening organ slipped out of her. He stood up and padded over to the window in his bare feet. Deborah followed him. Longarm pushed the curtain back a little so they could look out.

He frowned as he saw the group of men in front of the marshal's office. A couple of them carried torches, and one of them held a lantern aloft. Longarm was reminded of a lynch mob, and he thought they must have come to take Cy Torrance out of jail, drag him down to the river, and string him up from one of the cottonwoods, just like what had happened to Torrance's son.

And to Eph Bridges as well, recalled Longarm. And Barney Whitten, the hostler who had killed Sarah Gilley and started this mess, had hanged himself, but inside the livery barn rather than from one of the cottonwoods. Not to mention Tom Rankin, who had escaped from jail by pretending to take his own life by rigging a noose around his neck.

It was like a damn epidemic of hanging had descended on the settlement of Dry Creek.

But there wasn't going to be any more of it if Longarm had anything to say about it. He turned away from the window and reached for his clothes.

As he began drawing them on, Deborah said, "Custis, what should I do?"

"Get your little girl and go home," Longarm told her. "Stay there. Be ready for trouble." He paused to buckle on his gunbelt, then added, "And if you don't mind sending up a good word to El Señor Dios, a little praying might not hurt anything either."

Chapter 19

By the time Longarm reached the street, he could tell that the crowd in front of the marshal's office wasn't a lynch mob after all. Frank Webber himself was there, and he seemed to be doing most of the talking.

"If we sit back and wait for Torrance's men, they'll wipe us out, sure as shootin'," declared Webber. "Torrance is in there in the jail cell right now, boastin' that his foreman Jess Garth will go ahead and attack the town anyway, no matter what happens to him."

"But he'd be risking his own boss's life if he did that," protested one of the men. Longarm recognized him as the townie called Yates.

"Accordin' to Torrance, Garth knows he wouldn't care about that. He wants Dry Creek to pay for what happened to Harry, no matter what happens to him."

Longarm wasn't surprised by what Webber was saying, because Torrance had said pretty much the same thing to him. But he wasn't sure if it was a good idea for Webber to be out here stirring up the crowd like this. For one thing, Longarm wasn't sure that Jess Garth would go through with the attack, no matter what Torrance thought, and for another, even if Garth and the rest of the Rocking T men did try to carry out Torrance's vengeance plan, getting all worked up into a frenzy wasn't going to help the townspeople. They needed to stay cool and clearheaded if they were going to have any chance of defending Dry Creek.

"What do you think we should do?" another of the citizens asked Webber. None of them seemed to have noticed Longarm yet, and neither had the local lawman.

"I been sayin' all evening that we need to take the fight to them." Webber smacked his right fist into his left palm to emphasize the words. "Take 'em by surprise instead of sittin' back and waitin' for them to attack us. If we hit 'em hard enough, fast enough, we'll scatter 'em, and then we can send somebody to the county seat for help."

"Earlier, you said we ought to all go out and attack the Rocking T headquarters," said Yates.

Webber nodded. "Yeah, and that might've worked before Marshal Long grabbed Torrance and brought him back into town. Now Garth and the rest of Torrance's crew are waitin' not far outside of town, I'll bet, tryin' to figure out what to do. They'll never expect us to strike first."

The things that Webber was saying had some merit to them, and sometimes a bold stroke such as the one he described was just what was needed to turn around the odds in a bad situation. Longarm had pulled off many such daring stunts in his career as a lawman.

But so far during his time in Dry Creek, he hadn't seen anything to indicate to him that these folks were capable of doing such a thing. Torrance's cowboys weren't quite as salty as they were made out to be—Longarm had not only gotten out of Dry Creek, but he had also penetrated right to the heart of the Rocking T, captured Torrance, and gotten back here after all—but they were more than a match for a bunch of clerks and storekeepers.

Plus, if the men left Dry Creek and attacked Torrance's crew, they would be fighting out in the open, with no place to hole up if things went against them. The Rocking T gunmen might wipe them out, and then the settlement would be completely defenseless.

They needed to understand all this before they made up their minds what to do, so as the men muttered among themselves, Longarm raised his voice from the back of the crowd and said, "Hold on just a blasted minute! You folks have got a whole bushel of apples to eat, and you'd best do it one bite at a time or they'll all go rotten!"

They all turned to look at him, frowns of surprise and confusion on their strained faces. Webber exclaimed, "Marshal Long! I thought you'd gone to the hotel to get some shut-eye."

Longarm didn't explain that he had been awakened by Deborah Kane—and as it turned out, awakened quite pleasantly too. Instead, he said, "I got all the rest I need," which was stretching the truth more than a mite, since he was still tired. He went on. "You folks had better think twice about attacking Torrance's crew. I've tangled my twine with them a couple of times now, and I can tell you, they're a tough bunch. If you jump them out there on the prairie, you're liable to have more than you can handle."

"So what are you saying, Marshal?" demanded one of the townsmen. "We should just sit here and wait for them to ride in and kill us?"

"It ain't that simple a choice. I still hope I can talk some sense into Cy Torrance's head. Maybe he'll call off the whole thing."

Webber said, "It's too late for that. He's already a murderer. Don't forget poor ol' Eph Bridges."

Several men in the crowd cursed angrily at the thought of Bridges being strung up like that.

"Torrance claims that he didn't have anything to do with Bridges being lynched," said Longarm.

That brought expressions of scorn and disbelief from the crowd, and Webber said, "What in blazes did you expect him to do, Marshal? Of course he denied it."

"Oh, I don't know," drawled Longarm. "Torrance strikes me as the sort of fella who would tell you he'd done something and then spit in your face if you didn't like it."

That quieted them and brought back the frowns, as some of the men realized that what Longarm had just said was an accurate description of Torrance's arrogant personality. If he was really responsible for Bridges's murder, he would have been more likely to brag about it rather than deny it.

Yates scratched his head and admitted, "That *does* sound like Cy Torrance, all right. But if he and his men didn't kill Eph, who did?"

"I don't know," said Longarm. "Did he have any other enemies in town, somebody who might've grabbed a chance to get rid of him knowing that it would probably be blamed on Torrance?"

"Hell, everybody liked old Eph," said Webber. The other men nodded in agreement.

Longarm shook his head. "Somebody didn't. Either that, or they had some other reason for stringing him up."

Yates said, "I don't know who killed Eph, but we've got to decide what we're gonna do. Should we stay here in town and wait to see what happens, or should we try to hit Torrance's men first?"

Webber crossed his arms over his chest and glared. "I've told you what I think. Now it's up to you fellas to figure out what you think is best."

Yates looked at Longarm. "Marshal?"

"Wait," said Longarm. "Keep your guard up, and if Torrance's crew does attack, then fight like blazes. But at least you'll be fighting from inside the buildings. You'll have the stronger position."

Yates nodded and said, "That makes sense to me." He looked at the others. "What about the rest of you?"

The responses were mixed, but most of the men indicated that they were willing to wait awhile longer and see what happened. "I don't like having that threat hanging over me and my family," said one of the townsmen, "but I reckon if there's a chance to end this without a bunch of killing, we've got to take it." The man glanced at Webber. "Sorry, Frank."

Webber shook his head. "That's all right. You boys have to do what you think is best." He still looked like he disagreed with the decision, though.

The crowd began to break up. Longarm thought that was a good idea. He told the men to go back to their homes or businesses or wherever they wanted to be if an attack came, and to stay there and remain watchful.

Webber turned to go back into the office, and Longarm was about to follow him when a voice called, "Marshal Long! Marshal Webber!" Both men turned to see Deborah Kane on the porch in front of the café. She lifted a hand to summon them over and went on. "I've got coffee on to boil, and I'll have hotcakes and bacon ready in a few minutes too, if you're hungry."

Longarm realized as he heard those words that he was hungry. Downright famished, in fact, and the smell of coffee that drifted to his nostrils now was like a siren's call. He glanced at the sky and saw it turning gray with the approach of dawn. The sun would be up in a while, and if he wanted some breakfast, now was the time to get it.

"That sounds mighty good, Miz Kane," said Webber as he started toward the café. Longarm fell in step beside him.

Deborah must have gotten Lucy from the hotel lobby and gone the back way to the café, thought Longarm. He hoped that coming to see him in the hotel the way she had done wouldn't ruin her reputation. He hoped she was still alive after today to have a reputation to worry about. There was a good chance Everett would be discreet about what he knew. Most hotel keepers were fairly discreet, because it was good for their business to be that way. Plenty of things that folks didn't want their neighbors to know about went on inside the walls of a hotel, even in a little frontier settlement like Dry Creek.

They went into the café, and Deborah poured three cups of hot, fresh coffee that smelled like heaven to Longarm. She went to the kitchen to see about the hotcakes and bacon while Longarm and Webber sat at one of the tables. Deborah had lit only one lamp, so the place had a subdued, comfortable atmosphere about it, almost like they were in someone's home rather than a business.

"I'll just have this cup of coffee and then get back across the street to keep an eye on Torrance," said Webber. "He's still as full of poison as a rattlesnake. I never knew a man so eat up with hate."

"I'll join you," said Longarm. "I'd better tell Deborah to put our food on trays so we can take it with us." He smiled. "You need a good deputy to give you a hand, Marshal."

Webber grunted. "You applyin' for the job?"

"No, I've carried a badge for Uncle Sam for so long, I reckon I'm too set in my ways to ever do anything else. Although I'll admit that sometimes I think it might be nice to settle down and have a little spread somewhere."

Webber sipped his coffee and said, "I had a ranch once. Nice outfit, if I do say so myself. But I gave it up to pin on this badge, and I reckon I've done all right these past five years, even without no deputy. Town can't really afford to pay anybody else. My wages don't amount to much, but I don't need much to live, now that it's just me."

Longarm pushed his chair back and went over to the kitchen door, carrying his coffee with him. He pushed the door open with his foot and saw Deborah working at the stove. Lucy was asleep on a little cot on the far side of the room, bundled in a thin blanket since the early morning air was fairly cool.

Quietly, so as not to wake the little girl, Longarm said, "If you could put that food on a tray, ma'am, we'll take it with us. Marshal Webber and I need to get back over to his office."

"Are you sure?" asked Deborah. "I thought . . . maybe we could spend some more time together." She hastened on. "Not like before. I mean, just sitting and talking . . ."

Longarm smiled at her. In the blue gingham dress and the white apron, with her face a little flushed from the heat of the stove and a strand of dark brown hair that had come loose to hang over her face a little, he thought she was one of the prettiest women he had ever seen in his life. He would have thought that even if he hadn't bedded down with her a couple of times.

"I don't reckon there's a thing in this world that I'd enjoy more right now," he told her, and he meant every word of it. "But one way or another, things'll be coming to a head, and we can't leave Torrance unguarded. He's our ace in the hole. We shouldn't have left him alone this long already."

"Well, I know I've told you this several times before, but I'll say it again . . . be careful."

Longarm nodded.

Deborah piled a couple of plates high with hotcakes and bacon and placed them on a tray. As she handed it to Longarm, she said, "You and Marshal Webber can take your coffee with you. Just bring the cups back later."

"Yes'm," said Longarm as he placed his cup on the tray with the plates. He carried all of it out into the dining room, where Webber was getting to his feet.

"We're much obliged for this, Deborah," Webber told her. "If trouble breaks out now, you keep your head down and watch out for that little girl of yours."

"You can count on that, Marshal," she assured him.

Longarm and Webber went across the street. As Webber swung the door of the marshal's office open, a worrisome thought crossed Longarm's mind. The way things had been going, they were liable to find Cy Torrance hanged inside

137

the cell. There was a lot of that going around here in Dry Creek.

But Torrance was fine, Longarm saw to his relief. The rancher sat on the bunk inside the cell, glaring at them as they came in.

"Might as well let me out of here, Webber," snapped Torrance. "You're just makin' things worse for yourself and everybody else in this town."

"You've already threatened to wipe us out, Cy," Webber pointed out. "How much worse could it be?"

Torrance sneered. "You might be surprised."

The two lawmen sat down to eat their breakfast. Torrance watched them sullenly, and finally demanded to know when he was going to get fed.

"Later," replied Webber. "Assumin' your boys ain't killed us all by then."

When they were finished eating, Webber stood up and stretched, cracking some of the bones in his back.

"Been a long, hard haul," he said.

"You can go and try to get some rest if you want," said Longarm.

Webber shook his head. "No, I want to be here if trouble breaks out. Reckon I'll give myself a shave. That always wakes me up a mite."

He opened a door and went into a small room that contained a cot, a small table, a basin, and a mirror on the wall. Not very fancy, reflected Longarm, but he supposed it was home for Webber now that the marshal no longer had a ranch. Longarm lounged in the doorway to the marshal's living quarters and lit up a cheroot as Webber lowered his suspenders and took off his shirt, then lathered his face and started scraping off the silvery beard stubble. Like a lot of old-timers, Webber wore red, long-handled underwear, the top as well as the bottom, even though the weather didn't warrant it. The neck of the underwear came down fairly low in the back, and Longarm frowned as he saw a cross-hatching of white lines on Webber's skin. Those were scars, he realized. Quite a few of them, in fact.

He was about to ask Webber about them when rapid footsteps sounded on the planks outside. Longarm turned as the door into the office was jerked open and a man hurried in. Instinct sent Longarm's hand toward the butt of the holstered Colt, but he recognized the newcomer as one of the citizens of Dry Creek. The man had been among the crowd listening to Webber earlier, in front of the office.

Webber stepped out of the little bedroom with his shirt still off and lather clinging to his face in places. As he wiped a towel over his cheeks, he asked, "What's wrong, Carl? You came runnin' in here like a scalded dog. It ain't Torrance's men, is it?"

"Just one of them," replied the townie. "Jess Garth's ridin' into town, and he's got a white flag with him, like he wants a truce."

Chapter 20

Webber grabbed his shirt and shrugged into it as he and Longarm followed Carl back out onto the porch. The sun had started to come up, so there was a cheery orange glow in the eastern sky. The air was cool and pleasant. That would last for a little while, but as the sun rose higher, the heat would begin to build as well.

Jess Garth was mounted on a big chestnut horse that walked slowly along the street. He carried a Winchester with the butt resting against his thigh, and a white rag was tied to the barrel. It was a crude but effective version of a white flag.

Longarm and Webber strode out into the street as Garth reined in. Men had gathered on the porches and boardwalks along the street. Most of them held rifles or shotguns, and they looked like they would enjoy nothing more than blasting Garth out of the saddle. Longarm sensed that the whole town was ready to explode into violence at the slightest provocation, and he supposed that under the circumstances, he couldn't blame the citizens.

He wanted to hear what Garth had to say, though, and he was glad that the townies were restraining their bloodthirsty impulses, at least for the moment.

"How dare you ride right into town like this, Garth?" demanded Webber, his voice shaking a little with anger. "You're as bad as Torrance, think you own everything and everybody."

"You'd better set that old grudge aside, Webber," snapped Garth. "I'm here to do you a favor. I'm trying to save you and this town of yours from makin' a mighty bad mistake."

"And what mistake would that be?"

"Holding Mr. Torrance hostage. You'd better release him to me now. I've had all I can do to keep the boys from riding in here and burning this place to the ground. Sooner or later, I won't be able to stop them, and they'll do it if you don't let Torrance go."

"You mean they'll do what Torrance already threatened to do to us anyway?" Webber shook his head. "You ain't makin' a very good case, Garth. Seems to me like you're sayin' that we're damned if we do and damned if we don't." The marshal spat into the dust of the street. "Only difference is, if we hang onto Torrance, we can make sure he dies too."

"Nobody has to die," said Garth. "Let him go, and I'll talk him out of that crazy scheme."

Longarm knew from his visit to the Rocking T the night before that Garth wasn't completely sold on Torrance's idea of destroying Dry Creek and everybody in it. Garth had a good reason for not wanting to go along with that. Sooner or later, the authorities were bound to find out about it, and anyone who had taken part in such a massacre would be facing either a hangman's rope or life as a fugitive.

For that reason, Longarm believed what Garth was saying, but he wasn't confident that the foreman would be able to put a stop to Torrance's plan. Some of Torrance's gun wolves would probably be more than happy to take Garth's place, and if Garth got in Torrance's way, the vengeance-crazed cattleman would just have him gunned down.

Webber shook his head and said, "Torrance ain't goin' anywhere. He's locked up in my jail, and he's gonna stay there until you and the rest of the Rocking T crew go on back out to the ranch and leave us alone. You'd better splice that telegraph wire back together before you go too. As soon as I've been in touch with the county sheriff's office and told him what's been goin' on here, then I'll think about lettin' Torrance go."

Garth didn't say anything for a long moment, and Longarm could tell that he was considering Webber's offer. But finally, he shook his head and said, "The rest of the boys won't go along with that. The boss promised them a big payoff for taking care of this town, and they won't give up the chance of that."

Longarm spoke up, pointing out, "Torrance can't pay anybody off if he's dead, and that's what'll happen if his men attack Dry Creek."

Garth scrubbed a hand over his face and sighed. "I thought of that. If the boss is dead, and the town's destroyed, that bunch will scatter to the four winds . . . but not before looting everything they can from the Rocking T, including every head of stock on the place. They'll get their payoff, one way or the other."

"Sounds to me like you're starting to realize that you coiled your twine right in a bed of rattlesnakes, Garth," said Longarm.

The foreman grunted. "Maybe. But it's too late to change anything now."

"Includin' Torrance's mind," said Webber. "So you might as well turn that horse around and ride outta here, mister. If you're smart, you'll go another direction and keep ridin'."

Garth shook his head, his expression solemn. "I wish I could, Marshal. I really do. But that's not going to happen either."

Garth pulled the chestnut around and heeled it into a

trot. Several of the armed townsmen started to lift their rifles, but Webber motioned for them to stop. "Let him go," he called. With obvious reluctance, the men complied.

Webber kept the expression of angry, stubborn determination on his face until he and Longarm were back on the porch in front of the marshal's office. Then he frowned and said, "You reckon they'll attack anyway, like Garth said?"

"Now that they've figured out they can make a profit either way, I reckon it's a lot more likely," replied Longarm. "I was hoping that wouldn't occur to them. Should've known better. Hard cases like that always know where the money is."

"How long you think we've got?"

Longarm shook his head. "Hard to say. Garth might be able to hold them back for a while. They might even want to wait until nightfall again."

"That'd give us a chance to jump them first, like I've been talkin' about."

"This is your town, Marshal," said Longarm, "but I still think that's a bad idea. It's up to you and the citizens, though."

Webber sighed. "Damn, I wish Barney Whitten had kept his hands off that poor girl. If he hadn't killed her and then pretended to find her like that, then Harry Torrance never would've got blamed for what happened. Sure, Cy Torrance has run roughshod over people around here for a long time, and somebody should've put him in his place years ago, but at least the way things were, the town and the Rocking T sort of got along. Now the town's maybe doomed, and a lot of folks' lives are ruined."

"Including Cy Torrance," said Longarm. "He lost a son. That's a harsh punishment, no matter what he's done in the past."

"He had it comin'," barked Webber. "Don't waste any time feelin' sorry for Cy Torrance, Marshal."

Longarm shrugged. He said, "I've slept since you have.

144

Why don't you get some shut-eye? Shaving can't replace sleep."

"Maybe you're right," allowed Webber. "I can lay down for a spell anyway, I reckon. I'll go over to the hotel and see if Everett will let me have a bed for a while." He smiled humorlessly. "That cot in the back room ain't all that comfortable."

Longarm nodded and said, "Go right ahead. I'll hold down the fort here, and if Torrance's men *do* attack, there'll be enough commotion to wake you up."

"Yeah, I expect you're right." Webber extended his hand. "If we don't see each other again, Long, I just want to say it's been a pleasure knowin' you, even if it ain't been for very long but under hellaciously bad circumstances."

Longarm shook hands with the local lawman and nodded. Webber started along the street toward the Plaza Hotel.

Longarm opened the door of the marshal's office and went inside. From the cell, Torrance demanded, "What the hell happened out there? Where's Jess?"

"Gone," replied Longarm. "He wanted us to let you go. Said if we did, he could talk you out of what you've got planned for Dry Creek."

Torrance snorted. "No chance of that."

"Why not?" asked Longarm. "If you really didn't have anything to do with hanging Eph Bridges—and I don't think you did—then you're not really guilty of anything except shooting your mouth off and having a telegraph wire cut. That's not going to land you in prison or on the gallows. Wiping out this town will. Hell, in a case like that, the law might even send the army in after you."

"You think I care?" shot back Torrance. "You still don't understand, mister. I'd rather be dead than let my son go unavenged. I'd hang a dozen times over, as long as I got to settle the score first."

Longarm looked at him for a second, then said in a hard

voice, "You're right, Torrance. I don't understand a man like you. I don't reckon I ever will."

He turned away from the cell, went to the desk, and sat down. Fishing out a cheroot, he lit it and smoked in silence for several minutes, blowing smoke rings into the air as he always did when he was in Billy Vail's Denver office. He sort of wished he were there right now, swapping yarns with Vail or pestering Henry, the four-eyed young gent who played the typewriter in the chief marshal's outer office.

Longarm felt his eyelids growing heavy as he leaned back in the chair. The few hours of sleep he had managed to get during the past few days had been welcome, but they hadn't done much to restore his strength and energy. He was still operating on the reserves contained in his rangy, powerful body. Sooner or later, those would run out.

Longarm didn't think he would have to worry too much about that. Torrance's men would attack before that time came. He felt sure of it. Like Webber had said, if only Barney Whitten had kept his hands off Sarah Gilley. If only the hostler had been able to restrain his lustful impulses, if only he hadn't panicked and beaten poor Sarah to the point of death once he realized what he'd done to her, everything would be different.

Everything . . .

With that thought in his mind, Longarm dozed off. He didn't mean to, and he wasn't even aware of it when it happened, but there it was anyway.

He jerked awake, unsure of how long he had slept. A glance at the window told him that the sun was shining brightly outside. An hour, maybe more, had passed.

Longarm's heart slugged hard in his chest. A loud pulse echoed inside his head. The wheels of his brain turned, revolving so fast that they seemed to blur like the wheels of a racing stagecoach.

146

Everything was different.

And as he thought about all the things he had seen and heard for himself and all the things he'd been told about what had happened in Dry Creek before his arrival in the settlement, he knew it was true. It was like looking at a picture and seeing one scene, then standing it on its end and realizing that there had been another scene there all along, staring him in the face.

All it took to understand that was the idea that one lie could change everything.

Longarm came to his feet. He didn't know whether to grin or curse. He had a theory and he had a few facts that supported it, but nothing in the way of real proof, nothing that would stand up in a court of law.

Of course, there were more pressing problems than proving something in court. Nobody would ever stand trial for anything that had happened previously in Dry Creek if the town was wiped out by the crew of gun hawks from the Rocking T. Longarm swung toward the cell and said, "Torrance!"

The vengeance-crazed rancher was leaning against the back wall of the cell, his eyelids heavy as he dozed. He came awake with a start at the sudden urgency of Longarm's voice. Blinking, he shook his head and said, "Wha . . . what the hell?"

Longarm went to the barred door. "Listen to me, Torrance. You've been wrong about what happened here. So have I."

"Wrong?" Torrance repeated with a confused, angry frown. "You mean about what happened to Harry? My boy's dead, Long! I buried him next to his ma. How could I have made a mistake about that?"

Longarm nodded and said, "Yeah, Harry's dead, and I sympathize with your loss. I really do. I didn't know your son, but I know he didn't deserve to be lynched like that.

147

But it's the reason behind it all that I didn't figure out until now."

Torrance shook his head. "These damn townies wanted to get back at me, that's the reason. Oh, they fooled themselves into thinking that they were just dealin' out justice for what happened to that girl, but really it was because they hate me and resent me."

"You're wrong about that. But they were wrong too. They blamed Harry for Sarah Gilley's death."

"And Barney Whitten really killed her, I know. You think that makes things any better, to know my boy died for no good reason at all?"

"There was a reason," said Longarm. "But not the one that everybody in town believed. Everybody but one man."

Torrance came to the door and gripped the bars, hard. "Damn it, quit talking in riddles," he grated. "If you know something, spit it out."

"I know who was responsible for everything that's happened here in the past week. But before I tell you, you've got to give me your word that you'll let the law handle it. You'll call off your men and leave the town alone."

Torrance glared at him for several seconds, then said, "You're claiming that one man caused everything? That girl's death, Harry's lynching, what happened to old Eph Bridges?"

Longarm nodded. "That's right."

"One man didn't hang my boy."

Longarm couldn't deny that. "The law will deal with the folks who were part of that lynch mob too," he said. "But the hombre who planned it all out is the one you really want, ain't he?"

Torrance's breath hissed between his gritted teeth. "Give him to me," he said after a moment. "Give me that man, and I'll leave you and your blasted law to take care of the lynch mob."

Longarm thought about it, and at that moment he

148

couldn't have honestly said whether he wanted to make that deal or not. One man's life against the life of a town . . . It was a tempting bargain, even if it went against the rule of law.

But he didn't have to make that decision, because an instant later a volley of gunshots roared out somewhere in Dry Creek, and people in the street began to scream.

Chapter 21

Longarm whirled around. As he started for the door, Torrance called after him, "Long! Let me out of here! I'll help you!"

Longarm kept going. He didn't trust Torrance enough to accept the offer. If the gunnies from the Rocking T were attacking the town, Longarm might free Torrance in the hope that he could call them off, but otherwise, Longarm would deal with this new threat himself.

He snatched a Winchester off the rack before he ran out the door. The shots had stopped, but that didn't mean they wouldn't start again at any second. As he emerged from the marshal's office, he lunged to the right, recalling that there was a water barrel down there at that end of the porch.

The move was a good one, because even as he made it, another shot rang out and a bullet whistled past his ear to thud into the wall of the building. Longarm dived behind the barrel. From the corner of his eye he had seen a puff of powder smoke jet out from the roof of the hotel, behind a decorative railing that ran along the front of it. As he pulled himself up into a kneeling position behind the barrel, two more shots blasted out and the bullets hit the barrel. The rainwater collected inside it stopped the slugs before they penetrated to the other side.

Longarm flicked a glance up and down the street. It was deserted. Everyone who had been out here had scurried for cover when the shooting started. Probably there hadn't been very many people on the street anyway, because everybody was lying low, waiting to see what Torrance's men were going to do. Longarm had worried that he would see a few bloody corpses sprawled in the dust when he came out of the marshal's office.

The bushwhacker on the hotel roof hadn't killed anyone yet, more than likely because he had been trying to lure Longarm out of the marshal's office so he could get a clear shot at the big lawman. That was the way it seemed to Longarm anyway. He had been wearing a target on his back without knowing it ever since he'd ridden into Dry Creek. The killer had bided his time, but finally lost patience. To his way of thinking, he had to make sure that Longarm died. He couldn't leave that to chance.

Longarm thrust the barrel of the Winchester around the side of the water barrel and triggered three shots as fast as he could work the rifle's lever, spraying the lead along the railing on the hotel roof. He didn't figure he would actually hit the bushwhacker, but he wanted to make the son of a bitch duck. Then, as soon as the third shot roared out, Longarm was on his feet again, springing out from behind the barrel and racing across the street toward the hotel.

He heard shots but didn't slow down. The bullets were probably kicking up dust around his feet, but he didn't care how close they came as long as they didn't hit him. With a huge bound, he leaped from the street onto the hotel porch and rolled across it to come to a stop against the wall. He surged up, pressed his back against the wall for a second with the Winchester held slanted across his chest. He dragged in air to catch his breath after the run, then whipped through the double doors at the front of the hotel, shouldering them open with a crash as he charged into the lobby.

Longarm spotted the hotel keeper, Everett, crouching behind the desk, six-gun in hand. Thankfully, Everett wasn't trigger-happy and didn't start firing as soon as Longarm stormed in. Instead, he gasped, "Marshal Long! What's going on? Is it Torrance's men?"

"Not yet," snapped Longarm. "When they hear the shooting, though, they're liable to take advantage of the confusion and come on in. Stay here."

He headed toward the stairs that led to the second floor. As he reached the bottom of the staircase, Frank Webber appeared at the top, blinking and pawing the sleep out of his eyes with one hand while the other clutched a revolver. His shirt hung open, revealing the top of the red, long-handled underwear.

"Long!" he exclaimed. "What the hell!"

Longarm hesitated for a second, then pointed toward the roof with the barrel of the Winchester. "Somebody bushwhacked me!" he said. "Opened fire on people in the street to draw me out of your office."

"You hit?"

"Not yet," said Longarm as he started up the stairs.

Webber pulled back from the landing and waited as Longarm took the stairs three at a time. Then he waved the gun toward the end of the hall and said, "There's a ladder down there inside a closet, leads to a trapdoor that opens on the roof."

Longarm nodded. "Maybe we can get up there before he climbs down somehow."

As they hurried along the corridor, Webber said, "Sounded like a war bustin' out when that shootin' started. Made me jump out of bed like an earthquake had hit. I figured Torrance's men were attackin' the town, sure as anything."

"Not yet," Longarm said again. He didn't add the thought he had expressed to Everett downstairs, that the Rocking T gun wolves might try to take advantage of this opportunity to strike while the townspeople were distracted by other problems, but it was still a strong concern of his.

Webber jerked open a narrow door leading into a storage room. Past some stacked chairs, a table with a cracked leg, and several wooden crates, a built-in ladder led to a closed and latched trapdoor in the ceiling. A narrow, grimy window high on one wall let in a little light. Dust motes floated in the shaft of sunshine that slanted through the dirty glass.

Longarm headed for the ladder. He set the Winchester on the stack of crates, knowing that if he found what he was looking for on the roof he wouldn't need the rifle. The Colt in the cross-draw rig would be enough. Then he went hand over hand up the ladder, pausing at the top only long enough to throw back the rusty latch. It opened easily. He shoved the trapdoor up and scrambled through it onto the roof.

Like most Western buildings, the Plaza Hotel had a flat roof. Some had false fronts on them to make them appear more impressive, but the hotel already had a real second story, so the railing, which stood about four feet high, was the only decoration along the front. Longarm rolled to one side as he went through the trapdoor, palming out the Colt as he did so. As he came up on one knee, his keen eyes scanned the roof from one side to the other.

Empty.

That came as no surprise to him. The bushwhacker had had time to get down from his shooting perch up here. Longarm stood up and called to Webber, "He's gone."

Webber climbed out onto the roof, a disgusted look on his craggy face. "Must've put a ladder up against the back wall or something," he said.

Longarm strode in that direction. "Let's take a look."

Webber followed him. When Longarm reached the back of the hotel, he peered over the side and saw that a ladder stood there, all right, just as Webber had suggested. That was no surprise either. He said, "Yep, there's the ladder."

Webber had hung back a little, so that he was about ten feet behind Longarm. "See any tracks down there in the alley?" he asked. "Maybe we can follow the son-of-a-bitch bushwhacker."

Longarm moved as fast as he ever had in his life, turning and bringing up his Colt while Webber was still drawing a bead on his back. The local lawman froze. His gun was raised and pointing at Longarm, but he was also staring down the barrel of Longarm's Colt, and the icy expression in Longarm's eyes made it plain that if Webber pulled the trigger, he would die too.

"No, there are no tracks in the alley," said Longarm, "because the son-of-a-bitch bushwhacker is still up here."

Chapter 22

Webber's eyes widened. "What in blazes are you talkin' about, Long?" he demanded. "That killer's long gone! Put that gun down, blast it."

Longarm shook his head. "So you can go ahead and murder me like you did Eph Bridges? I don't think so."

"You're crazy! I was asleep downstairs when the shootin' started!"

"That's a lie, just like you've lied about everything else. You can't bluff anymore, Webber. I know what happened, and mostly I know why. I just couldn't prove it. That's why I came up here with you, to give you the chance to finish the job. And when I turned around, I saw exactly what I expected to see in your eyes. You were ready to kill."

Webber's gaze narrowed, and now his eyes were as cold as Longarm's. They were filled with hatred too.

"Damn it," he said. "Why'd you have to bring those prisoners up here? If you hadn't rode in when you did, everything would be fine now."

"You mean the town would be in ashes, everybody in it would be dead, and Torrance and his men would be hunted for the rest of their lives as killers. That's what would have happened."

"It still will," said Webber. "And you'll be dead too, so nobody will ever know what I did."

Longarm's hand was still steady as a rock as he pointed the Colt at Webber, despite the weight of the gun. The same was true of Webber. It was a contest of wills now. If either man's weapon drooped, the other would fire.

"Everybody will know," said Longarm. He wanted to get under Webber's skin, maybe spook the man into doing something foolish, like trying to get away. Then Longarm could wound him and take him into custody and maybe head off the attack by Torrance's men. "Everybody will know you murdered Eph Bridges, strung him up by the neck. And worse than that, they'll know you raped and killed that poor girl. That's what I can't quite figure out. You don't strike me as the sort of man who'd do something like that."

The muscles in Webber's throat worked as he swallowed hard. "I never meant to hurt her," he said. "Hell, the whole thing was her idea. Sarah come to me, said boys were always tryin' to get her to do things with them, and she was afraid she couldn't do 'em right. She . . . she said she wanted me to show her what to do, so's she'd know."

Longarm wasn't expecting that, but he kept his face stony as he said, "You mean you and her had been . . ."

"Yeah, for a while," admitted Webber. "A couple o' months maybe. But it wasn't my fault, damn it! Sarah . . . Sarah was a pretty girl, mighty pretty, and her body was built for lovin' even if her mind weren't. And my wife had been dead for years. It'd been so long since I'd been with a gal . . . Damn you, Long! Damn it, you just don't know what it's like!"

Longarm didn't want to know what it would be like to be Frank Webber. He didn't think he could stand having that many snakes squirming around inside his brain.

"What happened? Sarah wind up with child?"

"Nope." Webber shook his head. "She said she figured

she'd learned all she needed to from me, and now she could go and do it with all them young, handsome boys who'd been sniffin' after her, instead o' some old relic. But she was mighty grateful to me. Said she'd be sure and tell everybody I was the one who'd taught her to do it so good."

"And you couldn't let her do that, could you?"

"Hell, no! What do you reckon would've happened to me if everybody knew I'd been beddin' the gal? The whole town had practically adopted her! I'd've been tarred and feathered and run out of town on a rail, and that's if they didn't decide to go ahead and hang me!"

"So you tried to talk her out of telling anybody," guessed Longarm, "but you were mad and she got scared and ran away from you. You went after her and caught up to her and then *you* got scared, because even if she promised not to tell, she might forget by the next day and blurt it out to somebody. You realized what a big chance you'd been taking all along by getting involved with her, and you lost your head for a few minutes and started hitting her. You were mad too, because she wanted to go with other fellas and didn't want you anymore."

"I never meant to hurt her. I swear by all that's holy, I didn't. I thought . . . I reckon I thought that if we could just keep doin' it, me and her, that nobody would ever have to find out. I figured that there was really nothin' all that wrong with it." Webber's mouth twisted in a grimace. "Hell, she wanted it, and if it hadn't been me gettin' it, it would've been some damn cowboy. She was just a little idiot girl, and what I done to her never hurt a thing!"

"Until you beat her so bad she died," said Longarm. "You left her there in that alley, maybe thinking that she was already dead, and went back to your office. Must've been a hell of a shock when Barney Whitten came running in a few minutes later and said that he'd found her."

"Barney shouldn't have been there," snapped Webber.

"No way I could know that he'd stumble across her like that."

"You had to hurry back with him," continued Longarm, betting that he could hold his gun steady longer than Webber could. And the longer he kept Webber talking, the better the chance that would happen. "Did she really say Harry's name when you asked her who had done that to her?"

"She said it, all right. Whitten heard her. Like I told you, though, Long, I really think she was sayin' *hairy* with an *i*, because Whitten found her and he was a bushy son of a bitch."

"You didn't think of that until later. Right then, all you could think about was the fact that fate had given you the perfect opportunity to cover your tracks. Not only that, but you realized you could get back at the man you hated worse than anybody else in the world, Cy Torrance, by blaming what happened to Sarah Gilley on his son. You knew how Torrance doted on the boy, no matter what Harry was really like. You knew that Whitten had heard her dying words. You knew the town would believe that Harry Torrance was guilty. For all I know, you may have already been thinking about manipulating things so that folks would think they had to string Harry up in order to get any justice."

"Cy Torrance deserved to lose his boy! He had it comin'!"

"Why?" Longarm shot back. "Because he forced you off your ranch five years ago? Because he had you horse-whipped? I saw the scars on your back, Webber. I know what happened. Torrance even told me some about it."

Webber's voice was choked with emotion as he said, "Did the bastard tell you that my wife was buried on that ground? He didn't give a damn about that. He wanted the spread, so he had to have it. Never gave a second thought to what was right and proper."

But even though his voice shook, his hand was still steady on the gun that it held.

"That hate festered in you all this time, didn't it?" asked Longarm. "You never got over it. You blamed Harry for what happened to Sarah, and you got the citizens of Dry Creek to carry out your revenge on Torrance by lynching Harry. That was bad enough. But then you got the idea to twist the knife in Torrance even more. You figured out what Sarah said, and you realized it would hurt Torrance even more to know that his son died by mistake. Because even though Torrance loved Harry, in the back of his mind there had to be a little doubt. He had to have asked himself if maybe Harry really was guilty. You took that doubt away by shifting the blame to Barney Whitten. You went to the stable, made him write that note at gunpoint, then slugged him, put a rope around his neck, and hauled him up to strangle to death. Now the tragedy was compounded for Torrance. His son was dead, and there was proof Harry had been hanged for something he hadn't done."

"You're full o' words, ain't you?" asked Webber with a sneer. He had regained some of his composure and wasn't as shaken now. "Think you're so damned smart."

Longarm shook his head. "No, you're the one who thinks he's smart. You fooled Torrance, and everybody in town too. You might've let it end there and been satisfied with the grief you'd caused Torrance, but then he went loco and started threatening to wipe out the whole town. That worked out for you too."

"You're the one who's loco! How does it help me to get killed when Torrance's men attack Dry Creek?"

"You didn't plan to be here when the attack came," said Longarm. "You would've slipped out of town and let the people you swore to protect all be killed and the town be destroyed. You knew that once word of the massacre got out, Cy Torrance would be thought of as a mad-dog killer. He'd be the most wanted fugitive in the West. He'd lose his ranch and have to go on the run and sooner or later would wind up at the end of a hangman's rope. His life would be completely ruined, what was left of it."

An ugly grin stretched across Webber's face. He didn't bother to deny Longarm's theory. "Yeah, and I planned on bein' there when he was hanged too. I wanted him to see me in the crowd, smilin' up at him, and know that I was the one who'd done it to him, the one who'd caused him to be on that gallows. Would've been damned near the best moment of my life."

"Then I came along."

"Yeah." Webber snarled. "You came along and started tryin' to ruin everything. You kept talkin' about findin' some way to keep Torrance from attackin' the settlement."

"And that's not what you wanted at all. You wanted a massacre, so Torrance would be blamed for it. It was the same thing you did with Harry, only on a heap bigger scale. When I brought Torrance back from the Rocking T and threatened to upset that applecart, you started trying to goad the townspeople into attacking Torrance's men. You told them to strike first, knowing they'd be wiped out anyway. That's why Eph Bridges died. You wanted to spook the folks in Dry Creek into starting the ball, so you made it look like some of Torrance's gunnies had slipped into town and hanged Bridges. You wanted the rest of the men responsible for what happened to Harry to believe that they had to go along with your plan to attack first, or the same thing would happen to them."

"You make it sound like I'm some sort o' crazy man, stringin' people up and tryin' to sacrifice a whole town just to square things with Torrance."

"You said it yourself, Webber," replied Longarm. "That's pretty crazy, all right."

Webber glared at him. "How'd you figure it out about Bridges? Everybody else blamed Torrance."

Longarm realized that Webber was using the same

tactic that he was. Webber wanted him to keep talking so that his arm would get tired and let the Colt swing out of line, even for an instant. Longarm was younger and willing to bet on his own muscles, so he obliged the other man.

"First thing that struck me as odd was the way Bridges had a mark on his forehead where he'd been walloped. Nobody snuck up on him from behind to knock him out and then string him up. Whoever did it walked right up to him. I don't think he would have let any of Torrance's men do that . . . but he wouldn't think twice about it if you came into the barn and started talking to him."

"I kept thinkin' he'd turn around," said Webber, "but he didn't. Reckon I got too impatient."

"I suspect that's easy to do when you're waiting to kill a man," said Longarm. "The next thing that put me on your trail was that blaze-faced gelding Bridges let me use. You said something about it while we were walking up the alley, after Bridges's body was discovered. But the horse was tied up out on the street, and I hadn't said anything about getting it from Bridges. The only way you could've known what mount I was using was if you'd been somewhere around the stable and had seen me leading it out. I didn't really put that together at the time, but it was there in the back of my brain. Later, after I grabbed Torrance and told him what happened to Bridges, he seemed honestly surprised. Some of his men could've done it on their own, I suppose, but I was convinced Torrance hadn't ordered it."

"All that's mighty flimsy," said Webber with a shake of his head. "No judge or jury would ever believe it."

"You never know," said Longarm. "Once I put all the pieces together, it didn't take me long to realize that everything could have happened that way. And you were worried that I'd put those pieces together, so you let Tom Rankin out of jail to kill me."

Webber grunted in surprise. "What about the place on my head where he walloped me?"

"You mean where you walloped yourself, to make it look good. You let Rankin out of jail on the understanding that he'd get rid of me for you. You gave him a Greener and told him to wait in that room across the hall from where Mollie Bramlett was locked up. She was the bait. You knew that once I found out Rankin had escaped, I'd go check on her first thing."

"Rankin was a damned owlhoot! How do you figure I knew I could trust him?"

"You couldn't. But if you offered him a big enough pay-off, you thought there was a chance he'd go along with your plan, and he did. Of course, if he'd killed me, you would have turned around and killed him, just to cover your trail, but I reckon Rankin didn't think things through that far."

"You are one long-winded, deep-thinkin' son of a bitch," said Webber. "I'm thinkin' I ought to go ahead and shoot you, just to shut you up."

"You know if you pull the trigger, I'll put lead in you before I go down. And I don't miss what I'm aiming at very often, Webber."

"You're hard to kill, all right. I reckon I should've done it one of the other times I had the chance. Kept waitin' for a better opportunity, though, one where nobody would ever suspect me, in case some of the folks here in Dry Creek lived through everything."

"So you tried to draw me out and bushwhack me just now, since everything else had failed."

"Now that beats me. How in hell did you know somebody else didn't shoot at you?"

"I had already asked myself how the whole thing might fit together if neither Harry Torrance nor Barney Whitten killed the Gilley girl," explained Longarm. "Thinking about that made me wonder who else might have killed

164

her. All the other odd things I'd noticed started linking up in my head. So I was suspicious of you to start with. I had a theory but no way to prove it. You obliged me by trying to kill me. Then you pretended like you'd been asleep when the shooting started. When we went into that storage room where the ladder is, I saw the dust flying in the air. Somebody had disturbed it pretty recentlike. That was you, climbing up here onto the roof and then back down to put on your little show once I made it to the hotel porch and you couldn't draw a bead on me anymore. That latch on the trapdoor told me it had been used recently too. Most of it was rusty, but the rust had been knocked off the catch and it opened easily. It probably stuck when you tried to climb out that way, and you had to force it open."

"You're an eagle-eyed bastard, ain't you?"

"I just try to watch what's going on around me," said Longarm. "You tried to convince me the bushwhacker had come and gone on that ladder. You would've shot me while I was standing there looking over the edge and blamed it on some hidden gunman who didn't really exist."

"Why didn't I just shoot you while we were down there in the storage room if I'm that loco?"

"Because you're still smart enough to know that you'd have been the only suspect if I died down there. I had to be out in the open again, where anybody could've plugged me from a distance." Longarm chuckled coldly. "Like I said, the look in your eyes when I turned around gave you away, Webber, and you're not even trying to deny any of it anymore."

"Why should I bother denyin' anything? It's just your word against mine, and you'll be dead soon enough. For that matter, so will everybody else in this blasted town. Nobody in Dry Creek stepped up to help me when Torrance stole my ranch and whipped me. Bunch o' damned cowards. They felt sorry for me and gave me the job as marshal, but I didn't want their damn pity. They should've done somethin' when it would've made a difference."

Longarm heard the pain as well as the bitterness in Webber's voice, but he couldn't bring himself to sympathize with the man. Sure, Webber had probably gotten a raw deal, but he had turned right around and given an even worse one to a lot of folks, starting with Sarah Gilley and including Harry Torrance, Barney Whitten, and Eph Bridges.

No, if Longarm wound up putting a bullet through Frank Webber's brain, he wouldn't lose a minute's sleep over it.

"Now what?" rasped Webber after a moment. "I can keep up this Mexican standoff as long as you can."

Longarm heard a note of desperation in Webber's voice and knew that what he'd just said was bravado. Webber must have felt his control over his arm slipping. Longarm's own muscles were crying out in pain by now. He had distracted himself by laying out the whole thing for Webber, but now that was done. He couldn't hold up the Colt much longer.

But he wouldn't have to. Instead, he smiled and said, "You're going to jail and then the gallows, sooner or later, Webber. Might as well give up and save us all some trouble."

"Hell! Why should I do that when nobody's gonna believe your crazy yarn anyway?"

"They'll believe me, Frank," said Everett from the open trapdoor behind the murderous marshal. "I heard enough to know that you're not the man we all thought you were."

That was another reason Longarm had kept talking: He had heard faint noises from down in the storeroom as somebody entered it and started up the ladder, and he had drowned them out with his own voice so Webber wouldn't hear them. Everett had paused at the top of the ladder and listened as Webber admitted his guilt. Longarm had barely been able to see the top of the hotel proprietor's head.

Now, as Everett spoke and raised up so that he was halfway out of the trapdoor, Webber gasped in shock and his reflexes and instincts took over. He started to turn to face what his brain perceived as a new threat.

But the old threat was still there, in the person of Longarm. Webber jerked to a halt and tried to bring the gun back to bear on the big federal lawman, but Longarm was already in motion. He lunged across the gap between them and slammed his Colt against Webber's head, clouting him for real this time just like Tom Rankin supposedly had.

Webber went down like a puppet with its strings cut, out cold by the time he hit the planks of the roof.

"Thank God you were able to stop him, Marshal," said Everett. "I wouldn't have believed it if I hadn't heard it from his own mouth."

"Yeah, well, corralling Webber ain't our only problem," said Longarm. "We still got to deal with Torrance's men."

Everett's face was pale and scared. "I know. That's why I climbed up here. I just got word from the lookouts at the edge of town." He swallowed. "The men from the Rocking T are on their way, Marshal. They're coming to burn the town, and kill everyone in it."

Chapter 23

Longarm turned his head to gaze off to the north. With all his attention focused on Webber for the past few minutes, he hadn't been able to look in that direction. But now he saw the dust cloud boiling up and knew it came from the horses of the Rocking T gunmen as they charged toward Dry Creek. They hadn't attacked immediately after the bushwhack attempt Webber had made on him, but neither were they waiting for nightfall.

"Warn everybody in town—" Longarm started to say to Everett, but then the bell in the church steeple at the other end of the settlement began to toll. The word had already gotten around, and now anyone in town who didn't know the hard cases were attacking could hear that warning bell.

Longarm holstered his Colt and bent to grab the unconscious Webber under the arms. He began to drag the marshal toward the trapdoor.

"What are you going to do with him?" asked Everett, who climbed all the way out onto the roof and got out of the way.

"Lock him up," replied Longarm. "After all this, I don't want him getting away."

"I don't see what that matters if the town is destroyed."

"We've still got a hole card," said Longarm as he lowered Webber's feet through the opening and then shoved him through. Webber dropped limply to the floor below.

"What hole card?" asked Everett, starting to sound panic-stricken.

"Torrance," said Longarm.

He hurried down the ladder. Webber showed no signs of coming around, but Longarm didn't want the marshal regaining consciousness until he was safely behind bars in the jail. As soon as Everett came down from the roof, Longarm told the hotel keeper to pick up Webber's legs. Together, they carried him downstairs to the lobby and out onto the street.

People were running here and there, panicking. Longarm gritted his teeth in frustration. He couldn't let go of Webber, but as he and Everett carried the unconscious man toward the jail, he shouted, "Get inside! Get under cover, damn it!"

Some of the citizens heeded the order and ducked into nearby buildings. Others continued running around like chickens with their heads cut off. Longarm couldn't do anything about that until Webber was locked up, so he and Everett hurried on.

Torrance was at the cell door, gripping the bars. "What's all the yelling about?" he asked as Longarm and Everett came in carrying Webber. Then he stared at the marshal and added, "What the hell happened to him?"

Longarm and Everett lowered Webber to the floor. Without answering either of Torrance's questions, Longarm grabbed the ring of keys from the nail on the wall and swung toward the cell. As he unlocked the door, he said, "Get out of there, Torrance, but don't try anything. You ain't out of the woods yet, not by a long shot. Everett, keep an eye on him."

Blustering questions, Torrance emerged from the cell. Longarm dragged Webber inside. The local lawman let out a groan as awareness started to seep back in on his stunned brain. Longarm stepped out of the cell and clanged the door shut. Webber lifted his head, gave it a groggy shake, and opened his eyes to peer up through the bars at Longarm with a hate-filled stare.

"All right, Torrance, come on," said Longarm as he grasped the rancher's collar with his left hand. He filled his right with the Colt and dragged the complaining Torrance toward the door.

"Damn it, tell me what's going on!" demanded Torrance.

"The circus is coming to town," grated Longarm, "and you're the damn ringmaster."

Torrance grinned. "My boys are on their way in, aren't they? They'll burn this town down around your ears!"

"Not if you stop them."

"I won't. You can kill me if you want. Go ahead. But I won't say a word or lift a finger to stop them."

"We'll see about that," said Longarm.

He thrust Torrance through the door and onto the porch. The street was mostly clear now, and he was glad to see that. He waved and yelled at the few citizens who were still in sight, motioning for them to get under cover. They did so, leaving the wide, dusty main street of Dry Creek empty of life. Even all the horses that had been tied at the hitch racks had been moved into the livery stable.

Longarm shoved Torrance into the middle of the street, then stood there with his gun pointing at the cattleman's head. The men from the Rocking T couldn't miss seeing them when they rode in. That wasn't going to be very long now. Longarm could hear the rumble of rapidly approaching hoofbeats. He smelled the dust in the air and knew it had been kicked up by those hooves. A moment later, the first of the attackers came into view, boiling around a corner a couple of blocks away and wheeling their horses toward the center of town.

171

The men reined in sharply at the sight of Longarm and Torrance standing alone in the middle of the street. Shouted curses filled the air as the men behind the leaders had to haul their mounts to an abrupt halt.

Longarm looked for Jess Garth, but didn't see him. Torrance's foreman had been opposed to the attack. Either he had kept riding after his visit to town, or he had gone back and tried to persuade the others to abandon their plans. If that was the case, clearly he had failed.

Lifting his voice so that he could be heard in the sudden, strained silence, Longarm called, "You boys just hold it right there! I've got your boss here, and if you don't turn around and ride out, I'll put a bullet through his head!"

Several of the gunmen laughed, and one of them said, "That's a damn bluff! You're a lawman! You won't shoot him!"

"Don't be so sure about that, old son," said Longarm. "I'm just about pissed off enough to pull this trigger, badge or no badge."

Torrance yelled, "Don't listen to him! I want this town razed! I don't care if I live or die, as long as Dry Creek dies!"

"They don't care either, Torrance."

The rancher jerked his head around to glare at Longarm. "What are you talkin' about?"

"They get their payoff either way. Fact is, they might come out ahead if you were to die, because they'll loot everything they can get their hands on at the Rocking T, including all the stock you've got. They'll sweep that spread clean and then take off for the tall and uncut. The place'll fall into ruin, and nobody will be there to take care of the graves of your wife and son. *That's* what you've set in motion here, Torrance."

The muscles in Torrance's face worked as he thought about what Longarm had just said. From the look in his eyes, he was realizing that Longarm was right. Like ripples spreading out from a stone tossed in a pond, the repercussions of Frank Webber's evil had spread through Dry Creek and the surrounding area.

But Torrance's thirst for vengeance had been an even bigger rock, and the ripples from it threatened to become bloody, destructive waves that would have far-reaching effects. A flood of death and despair loomed over this town and everyone in it—including Cy Torrance.

The rancher twisted his gaze back toward his men and ordered in a hoarse shout, "Get out! Go back to the Rocking T!" His voice choked a little. "Maybe . . . maybe it ain't worth it after all."

Longarm didn't think there was much chance of that happening, and sure enough, the man who now seemed to be the spokesman for the gun wolves laughed and said, "It's too late for that, Torrance. Too late to stop anything now."

That was what Longarm expected. But his ploy had already achieved some results. The sight of Longarm and Torrance standing in the middle of the street had stopped the attackers in their tracks, as he had hoped it would. And the brief confrontation had given the defenders holed up in the buildings time to catch their breath, settle their nerves, and draw beads on the gun horde. Longarm sent up a quick prayer to El Señor Dios that that was what they had done, then bellowed, "Let 'em have it!"

Guns blasted from windows all along the street. The sharp crack of rifles, the heavy booming of shotguns, the rattle of pistol fire all blended into an ear-shattering roar. The citizens of Dry Creek weren't fighters by nature, but they had delved deep inside themselves and found the reserves of strength and determination they needed to become warriors, if only for a short time.

The storm of lead scythed into the gang of gunmen, who were already starting to open fire with the guns in their hands. Still holding Torrance by the collar, Longarm dashed for the jail, pulling the rancher along with him. Bullets ripped through the air around them, but none of the slugs found their mark. Under fire and trapped in the middle of the street as they were, the hard cases were hurrying their shots.

Everett threw the door of the marshal's office open and stepped out with his rifle to peg several shots at the gunmen. Longarm practically tossed the smaller Torrance through the door ahead of him and then dived after him. Everett grunted in pain and started to fall, but Longarm snagged his coat and jerked him back into the office. Longarm kicked the door shut and heard bullets thudding into it.

The left leg of Everett's trousers had a spreading bloodstain on it. Longarm yanked the hotelman's belt off, wrapped it around his thigh above the wound, and pulled it as tight as he could before knotting it into place. That would slow down the bleeding until Everett could get some medical attention.

"Give me a gun," said Torrance. "They got to be stopped. They've gone crazy."

"You made 'em that way," snapped Longarm.

Torrance's hands clenched into fists. "I was out of my head with grief. I know now I was wrong, Marshal. Lemme do something to make up for it."

Longarm hesitated, then picked up the rifle Everett had dropped and tossed it to Torrance, who plucked it out of the air and worked the lever.

Then he spun toward the cell, where Frank Webber stood wide-eyed, gripping the bars.

"You'll die anyway, Webber!" screamed Torrance as he brought the rifle to his shoulder.

But before he could pull the trigger, the butt of Longarm's Colt slammed against the back of his head, driving him to the floor, unconscious.

Webber's face was so pale he must have known that he had been staring death right in the face for a split second.

174

"I figured he'd try to pull something like that," said Longarm as he turned his Colt back around so that he was gripping the butt again. "Hate's got too strong a hold on him. He'll never get over it."

Webber turned his gaze toward Longarm. "Let me out o' here. I'll fight with you, Long. I swear it."

"I didn't believe Torrance, and I ain't gonna believe you," said Longarm as he turned away from the cell. He picked up the rifle and carried it to the window, which had already been shattered by bullets. Standing to one side, he angled the barrel out and drew a bead on one of the gunmen. As the Winchester cracked, the man tumbled out of the saddle and fell to the ground.

He joined a lot of others who were already there. Longarm figured the opening volley had cut down at least a fourth of the gunmen, maybe as many as a third of them.

But a lot of killers were left, and they were spreading out over the town now, as the one big battle deteriorated into a lot of smaller conflicts. Longarm heard the crackle of flames and smelled smoke and knew that at least one building was already burning. Fire was one of the greatest enemies of any frontier town. Even if the gunmen were all wiped out, Torrance might have his revenge yet. The fire could spread and destroy every structure in Dry Creek.

Longarm knew he had to go out there. He looked over at Everett, who had pulled himself into a sitting position and propped himself against the desk.

"If I help you over here to the window, can you lean against the wall and keep fighting?" asked Longarm.

Everett nodded. "Damn right I can. Just give me a hand, Marshal."

Longarm did so, lifting Everett and supporting him as the hotelman hobbled over to the window on his good leg. He got himself balanced and took the rifle Longarm handed him.

"What are you going to do?"

Longarm nodded toward the street. "Take the fight to those bastards."

Everett grinned, even though lines of pain were etched on his face. "Reckon it's a little too late to tell you to be careful, Marshal."

"Just a mite," Longarm replied with a chuckle.

He got a second six-gun from the desk and made sure both weapons were fully loaded, then went to the door with a gun in each hand and took a deep breath. He hit the door with his shoulder, knocking it open, and lunged out onto the porch with both guns blazing as a knot of several attackers rode past. Longarm's deadly accurate fire emptied their saddles.

He spun as shots roared to his right and bullets clawed past him. Two gunmen who had probably had their horses shot out from under them in the opening moments of the battle came at him on foot, flame spouting from the muzzles of their guns. Longarm dived to the planks, his Colts bucking and roaring as he fell. The killers were driven backward off their feet by the slugs smashing into their bodies.

But Longarm's guns were empty now. He rolled off the end of the porch and scrambled behind the water barrel to try to reload. Unfortunately, most of the water had drained out of the barrel through the holes that Webber had put in it earlier, during his bushwhack attempt on Longarm. The thick wood of the barrel stopped some of the bullets that struck it, but some of them punched all the way through. Before too much longer, the barrel was going to look like a sieve.

Longarm jammed the extra gun behind his belt and thumbed fresh cartridges into the one he had taken from one of Torrance's men when he escaped from the Rocking T. That had happened less than twelve hours earlier, but it seemed like days or even weeks in the past to Longarm. Tension, danger, and lack of sleep had drawn him up as

176

tight as he had ever been drawn. His jaws were clamped to-gether, and curses escaped between his clenched teeth. Rage boiled up inside him at the tragic twists and turns of fate that had brought Dry Creek to this point. He had to take a deep breath to steady himself as his hands began to shake a little. He finished reloading the first gun, then hol-stered it and shoved fresh cartridges into the second one.

Then he filled both hands again and stood up. He strode out into the street, firing left and right, first one gun and then the other, drawing a bead with one Colt as he was bringing the other down from the recoil that had forced it up. He supposed bullets were flying all around him, but he didn't care. He was sick of this, sick of the lust and greed and pride and downright evil that had brought folks to this point. It had to end, at least in Dry Creek and at least for now.

One after another of the surviving gunmen went down under Longarm's steadily blasting Colts. Then the hammer of his right-hand gun clicked on an empty chamber, fol-lowed a second later by the same sound from the other weapon. He stood there, his chest heaving, empty guns still leveled, pulse hammering in his head, and only as his madly slugging heart slowed and the crescendo in his skull quieted did he realize that an eerie silence had fallen over the settlement, a silence broken only by the crackle of flames. He looked around at all the bodies littering the street around him, bloody and still. At the far end of the street, the late Eph Bridges's stable burned, but so far the fire seemed to be limited to that one structure. Longarm saw townspeo-ple starting to emerge from the bullet-riddled buildings, their faces pale, their steps unsteady. He lowered his guns and shouted in a voice made hoarse by powder smoke, "Bucket brigade! Form a bucket brigade and get that fire out before it spreads!"

He had to yell several more times before the orders got through to the stunned brains of the citizens. Then they grabbed buckets and ran for the creek, and soon water-filled buckets were being passed along a line to be tossed on the flames consuming the stable.

Longarm turned and walked slowly toward the marshal's office. His arms hung at his sides, the empty guns still clutched in his hands. He hoped Everett was all right. For a townie, the hotel keeper had sand.

"Custis! Custis!"

Hearing his name being called, Longarm looked up and saw Deborah Kane running along the street toward the marshal's office. Her daughter Lucy trailed behind her.

"Oh, my God, Custis! You're hurt!"

Longarm glanced down at himself. Sure enough, there were several crimson stains on his shirt and trousers. He hadn't even been aware that he'd been hit. But he knew none of the wounds were serious, just creases more than likely, because all his muscles still worked.

He tried to tell Deborah he was all right, but before he could find the words, she had angled off the boardwalk into the street and into his arms. His embrace was awkward because he still held the guns in his hands, but he managed to pat his forearm against her back and say, "It's all right, Deborah. It's all over now."

Then Lucy Kane screamed.

Chapter 24

Longarm stiffened in shock as he looked over Deborah's shoulder and saw Frank Webber lurch through the doorway of the marshal's office and grab Lucy, who had stopped on the porch to watch her mother and Longarm embracing ten feet away in the street. Webber had a gun in his hand, and he pressed the muzzle against Lucy's head, the tip of the barrel disappearing into her thick blond curls.

Deborah twisted around and screamed too when she saw her daughter squirming in Webber's brutal grip. "Frank!" she cried as she pressed a hand to her mouth. "Frank, what are you doing?"

Longarm recalled that he and Everett were the only ones in Dry Creek who knew the true extent of Webber's villainy, and the fact that Webber was loose meant that Everett was probably either dead or unconscious inside the office.

"Settle down, Deborah," said Webber in a harsh voice. "I ain't gonna hurt your little girl unless I have to. But I ain't gonna let anybody stop me from gettin' out of here neither."

Deborah took a step toward them. "But Frank, you can't mean to—"

Longarm caught her arm to stop her. "Hold it, Deborah," he said. "Webber's desperate. It's a long story, but believe me when I tell you he's liable to do just about anything."

An ugly grin stretched across Webber's face. "Damn right I will. And it ain't my fault. You're the one who ruined everything, Long."

"Still won't take any of the blame, eh?" Longarm shook his head. "You're one pathetic son of a bitch, Webber." He moved to one side, taking it slow and easy. He wanted Deborah well out of the line of fire if anything happened. He wanted Webber to take that gun away from Lucy's head too, so he went on. "You took advantage of that poor little girl with the mind of a child, and then you killed her. You're about the sickest bastard I ever crossed trails with, and the most gutless too."

"Shut up!" grated Webber. "You don't know nothin' about it."

"I know you're lower than a snake. Lower than a hydrophobic skunk. I'll bet if that wife of yours knew what you turned out to be, she'd be glad she was dead and gone before she ever had to see it with her own eyes."

"You leave my wife out of this, damn you!" yelled Webber. His face was flushed a dark red now.

"Hanging's too good for you, Webber. You ought to be shot down like the mad dog you are."

Longarm was all too aware that both of the guns he held were empty. He knew too that with all the commotion of the burning stable going on at the other end of town, the citizens of Dry Creek who had survived the battle with Torrance's gunmen weren't even aware of this deadly confrontation. But as he edged closer, he thought that if he could just draw Webber's fire, Lucy would have a chance to get free. Longarm figured he could close the distance between him and Webber in a couple of bounds, even with a bullet in him, and he could club the crazed marshal to death before he died himself. All he had to do was prod Webber a little more . . .

"Yeah, you're the sorriest excuse for a human being I ever saw, old son. You're lower than something I'd scrape off my boot heel. And I'll bet you weren't even a very good lawman."

"That's a damned lie!" howled Webber. "I gave this town everything I had, even after everybody in it turned their backs on me!"

And with that, he jerked the gun away from Lucy's head and pointed it at Longarm, ready to shoot him down in a frenzied rage.

Even as Longarm tensed in a probably futile effort to dodge the bullet, a rifle cracked somewhere behind Webber in the office. Webber was thrown forward by the slug crashing into his back. Deborah and Lucy both screamed. Webber let go of Lucy as he staggered forward a step. She sprinted to her mother. Webber's free hand caught hold of one of the posts supporting the awning over the porch. He twisted around and swung the gun up as Cy Torrance stepped out of the office, a rifle in his hands. The rifle blasted again, but Webber fired at the same time. Torrance's second bullet ripped through Webber's body and turned him halfway around at the edge of the porch. The slug from Webber's gun punched into Torrance's midsection. Webber swayed, but managed to stay upright long enough to jerk the trigger twice more. Both of those shots drove into Torrance's chest and flung him against the wall. Webber toppled over backward into the street as Torrance slowly slid down the wall, leaving a crimson smear on the boards behind him.

Deborah caught Lucy up in her arms and turned away from the gruesome scene, shuddering. Longarm stalked over to Webber and kicked the gun well out of reach, but it didn't really matter. Webber's glassy eyes stared sightlessly up at the blue morning sky. Longarm turned away from him and went to the porch, where Torrance sat hunched over against the wall beside the door. The rancher was still alive, but the blood-soaked front of his shirt testified that he wouldn't be for long. With an effort, he raised his head to look up at Longarm with pain-wracked eyes.

"Was it worth it, Torrance?" asked Longarm.

"I smell . . . smoke," rasped Torrance. "The town is . . . burning?"

"That fire's out." That was stretching the truth a mite, but a glance at the stable told Longarm that the townspeople were bringing the blaze under control. Dry Creek wasn't going to burn to the ground, at least not today. "More than likely what you're smelling is brimstone."

Torrance's eyes widened. He opened his mouth, probably in an attempt to gasp out a last curse, thought Longarm, but the only sound that came from his throat was the rattle of his final breath as death claimed him.

Longarm turned away, sickened by the sight of Torrance's corpse. But there was Webber, lying in the street, another reminder of the tragedy that had befallen Dry Creek. A bitter taste filled Longarm's mouth, like sour defeat under his tongue. He shook his head and stepped away from the bodies of the two men who had brought down so much death and destruction on the settlement. He didn't look back as he walked into the street. Instead, he kept his eyes fixed on Deborah Kane and on the little girl she carried in her arms, the morning sun bright on Lucy's fair hair.

The attack on Dry Creek by Torrance's men cost fourteen citizens their lives. Nine were killed outright in the fighting; five died of their wounds over the next few days. But forty-seven of the gunmen lay dead, an incredible total under the circumstances. The others had fled, and would probably never show their faces in this part of the country again.

Everett was alive. Frank Webber had just knocked him

out. Webber had had an extra key to the cell in his pocket. He had waited until the battle was over to let himself out, not wanting to venture into the street while so much lead was flying around, then clouted Everett, gotten hold of a gun from the desk, and opened the door to find a perfect hostage waiting there in the person of Lucy Kane. What he hadn't counted on was Cy Torrance regaining consciousness behind him and getting his hands on the rifle Everett had been using.

Eph Bridges's livery stable was destroyed, but the horses had broken out through the doors of their stalls before the flames reached them, and the blaze hadn't spread to any of the other buildings. Most of the businesses had bullet holes in their walls, but those could be patched. So could all the minor wounds that had been suffered, including the handful of bullet grazes on Longarm's body. He would be stiff and sore for a few days, but as soon as the telegraph wires were fixed, he intended to wire Billy Vail and let the chief marshal know that he would need a week or two to recuperate before he returned to Denver. Vail might not like the delay, but for once Longarm didn't really care. This little dustup had taken so much out of him that he really needed his rest.

So as soon as he was confident that everything in Dry Creek was under control, he crawled into a bed in one of the Plaza Hotel's rooms and slept the clock around. More than that actually, since dusk was settling down over the town on the day after the battle before he woke up again.

What finally roused him from the deep, deep slumber was the warmth of Deborah Kane's naked body pressed up against the battered length of his body.

He groaned and rolled over onto his back, and her lips found his. She kissed him long and hard, and when she finally took her mouth away, she whispered, "I know you've been through a lot, Custis, but you don't have to do anything. Just lie there. I'll take care of everything." Her hands

183

caressed him, coaxing life back into him. She moved above him, settling down so that the heat of her body engulfed him. He took refuge within her, letting her tenderness wash away all the aches and pains and bitter memories. This day might be done, but the world was made new again by their joining.

Longarm had never been the sort of hombre who wasted a lot of time looking back anyway. He was more interested in where the next trail would lead than in where he had been.

So he let out a booming laugh, rolled over to bring Deborah underneath him, and launched into a gallop, riding hell-bent for leather toward tomorrow.

Watch for

**LONGARM AND THE
HEIRESS**

the 351st novel in the exciting LONGARM
series from Jove

Coming in February!

GIANT-SIZED ADVENTURE FROM AVENGING ANGEL LONGARM.

BY TABOR EVANS

2006 GIANT EDITION

LONGARM AND THE OUTLAW EMPRESS
978-0-515-14235-8

2007 GIANT EDITION

LONGARM AND THE GOLDEN EAGLE SHOOT-OUT
978-0-515-14358-4

penguin.com

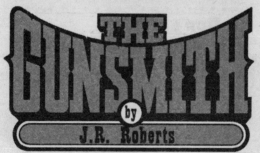

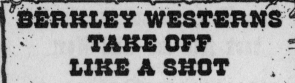